2 GRRRLS™

Locker Talk

Cool School Comics

by Holly Kowitt

SCHOLASTIC INC.

New York   Toronto   London   Auckland   Sydney

Mexico City   New Delhi   Hong Kong   Buenos Aires

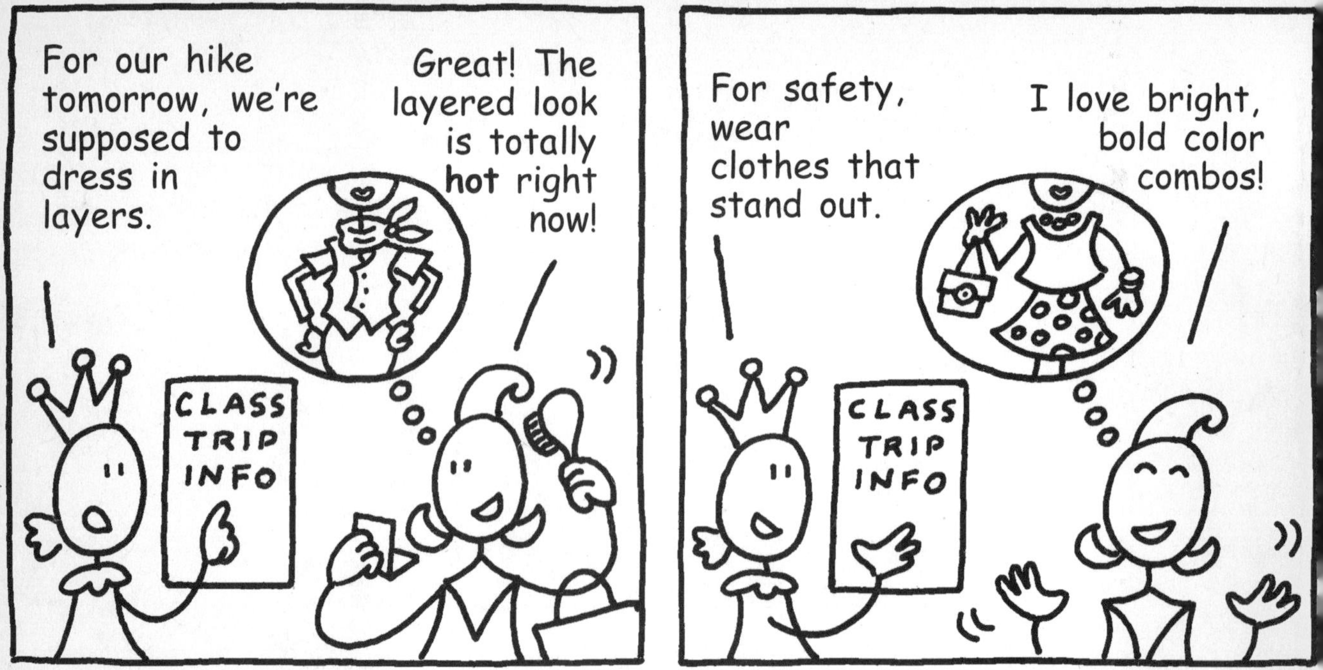
For our hike tomorrow, we're supposed to dress in layers.
Great! The layered look is totally **hot** right now!
CLASS TRIP INFO
For safety, wear clothes that stand out.
I love bright, bold color combos!
CLASS TRIP INFO

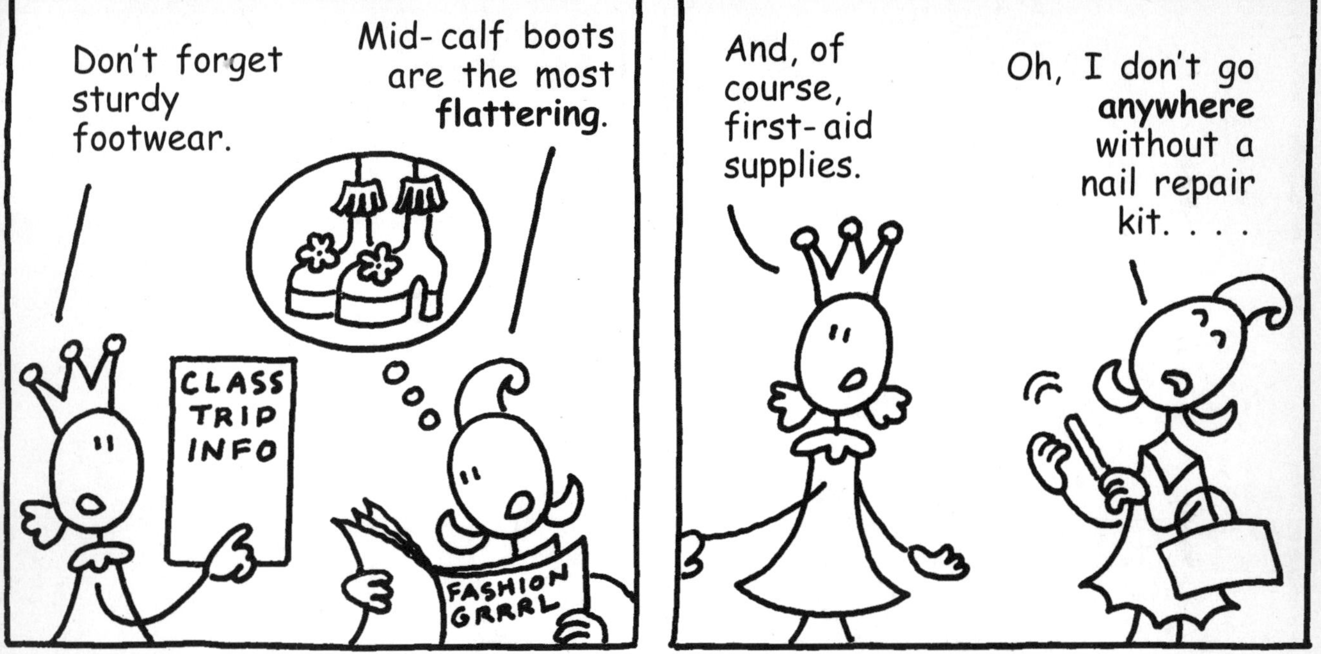
Don't forget sturdy footwear.
CLASS TRIP INFO
Mid-calf boots are the most **flattering**.
FASHION GRRRL
And, of course, first-aid supplies.
Oh, I don't go **anywhere** without a nail repair kit. . . .

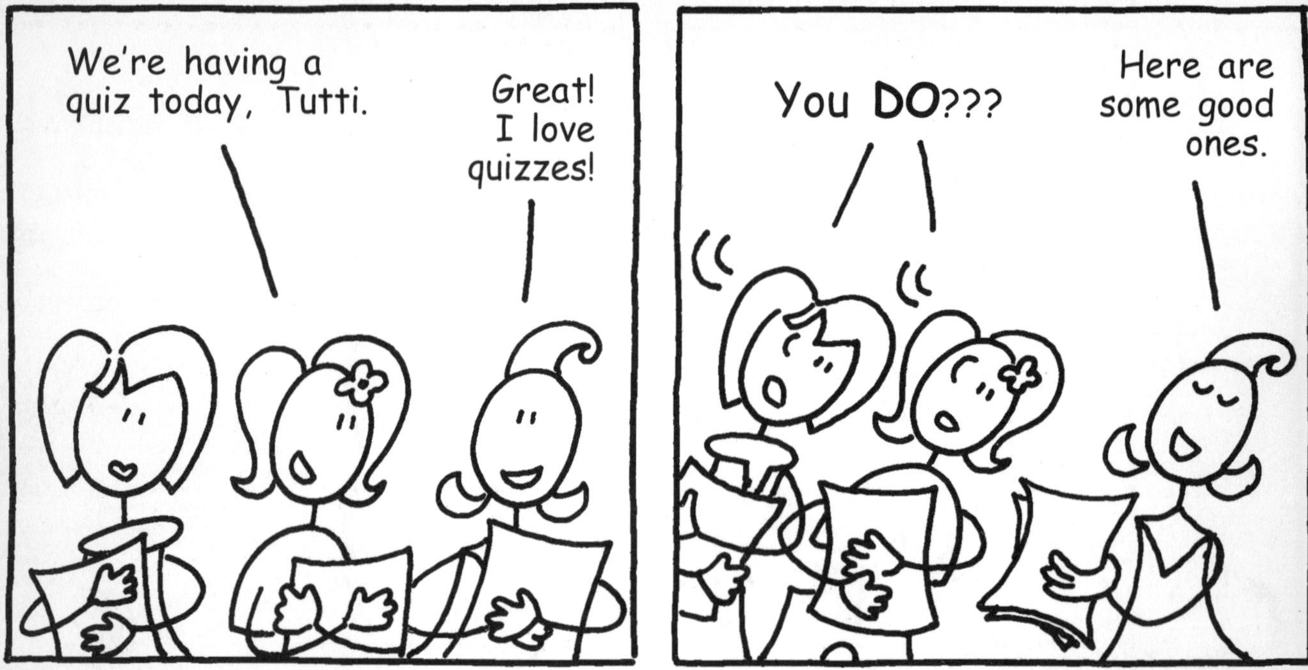
We're having a quiz today, Tutti.
Great! I love quizzes!
You **DO**???
Here are some good ones.

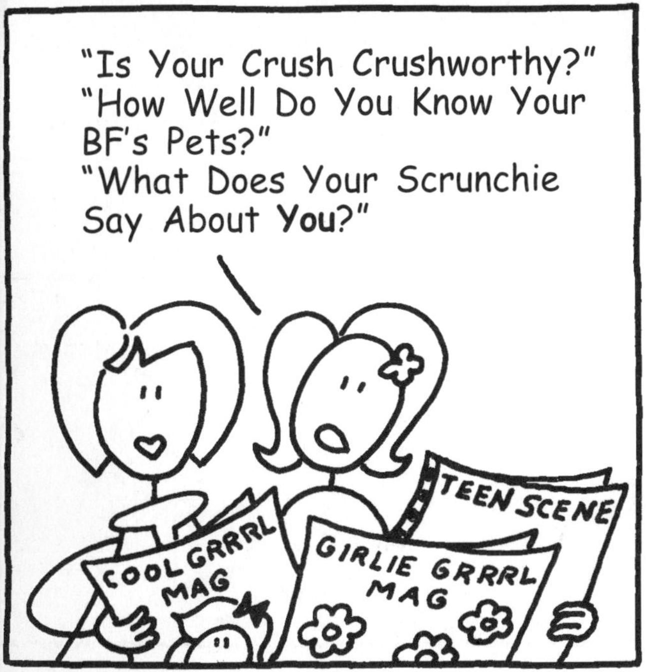
"Is Your Crush Crushworthy?" "How Well Do You Know Your BF's Pets?" "What Does Your Scrunchie Say About You?"
TEEN SCENE
COOL GRRRL MAG
GIRLIE GRRRL MAG

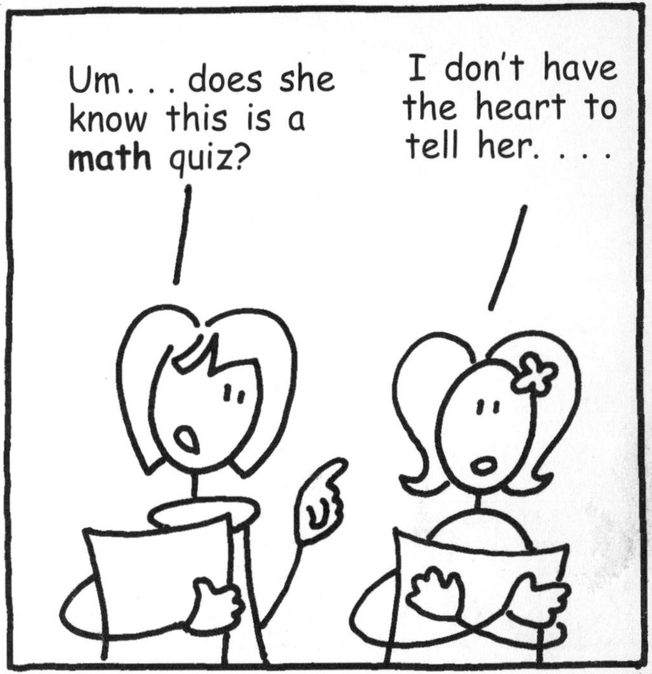
Um. . . does she know this is a **math** quiz?
I don't have the heart to tell her. . . .

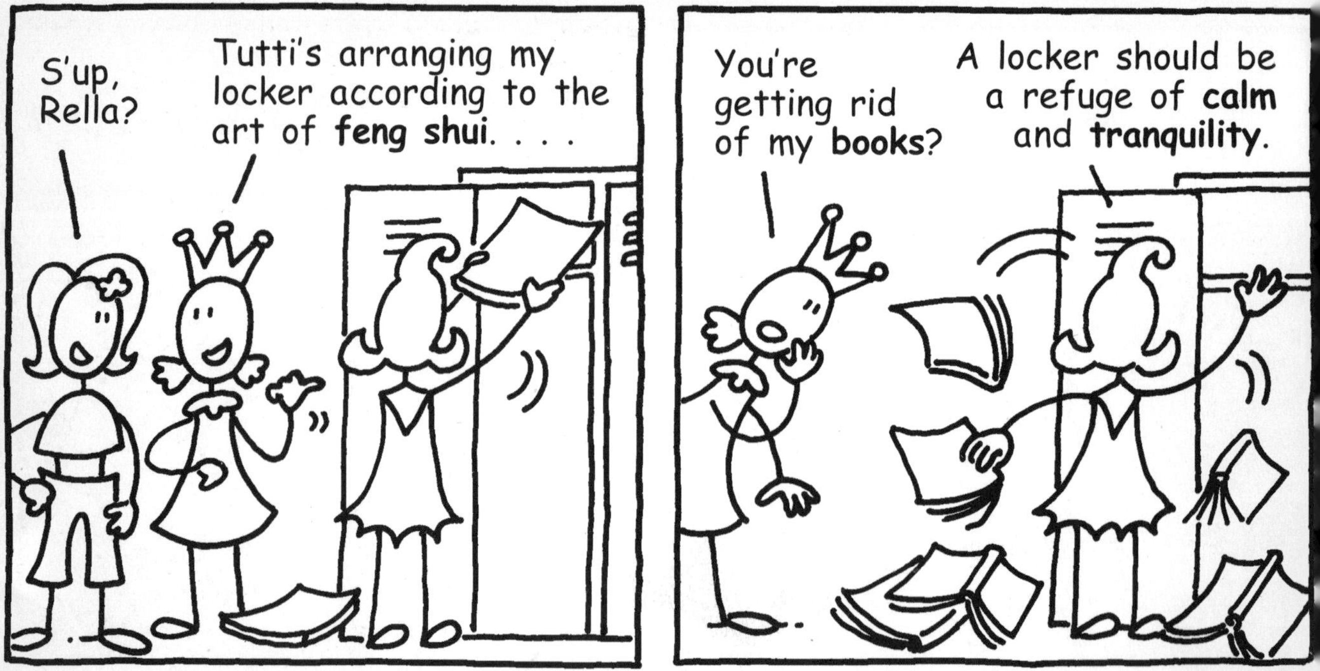
S'up, Rella?
Tutti's arranging my locker according to the art of **feng shui**. . . .
You're getting rid of my **books**?
A locker should be a refuge of **calm** and **tranquility**.

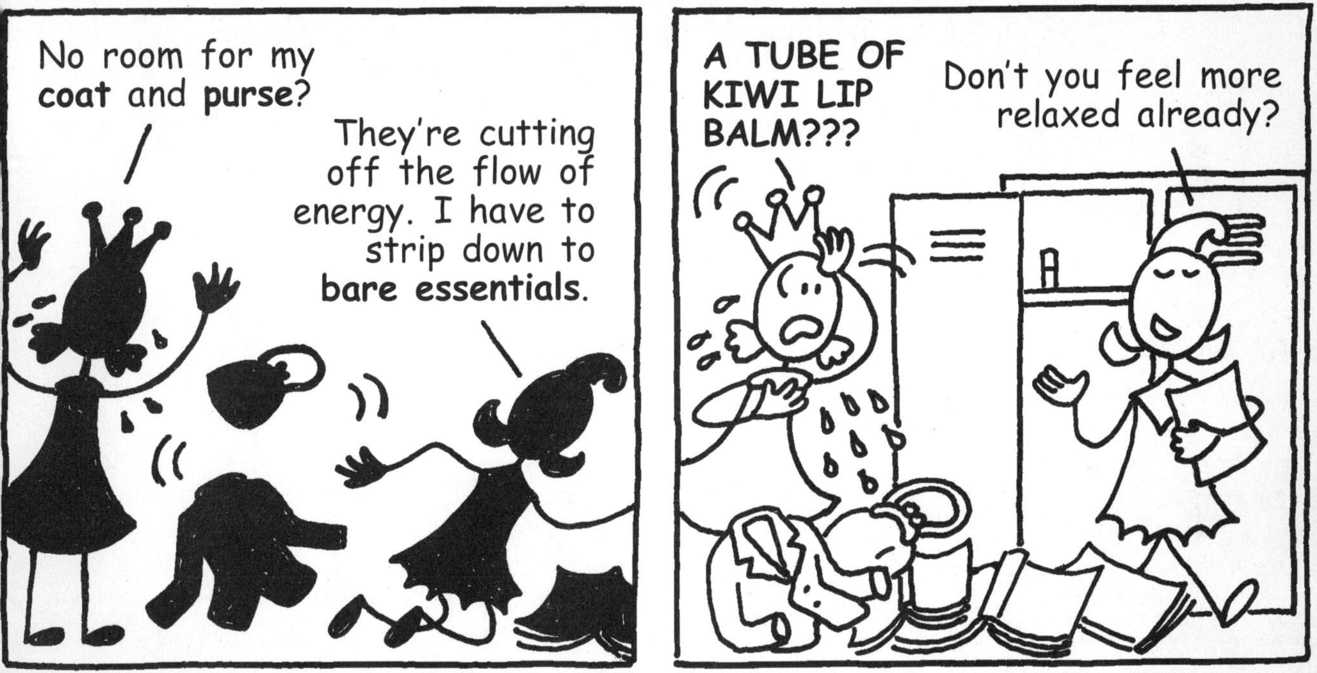
No room for my **coat** and **purse**?
They're cutting off the flow of energy. I have to strip down to **bare essentials**.
A TUBE OF KIWI LIP BALM???
Don't you feel more relaxed already?

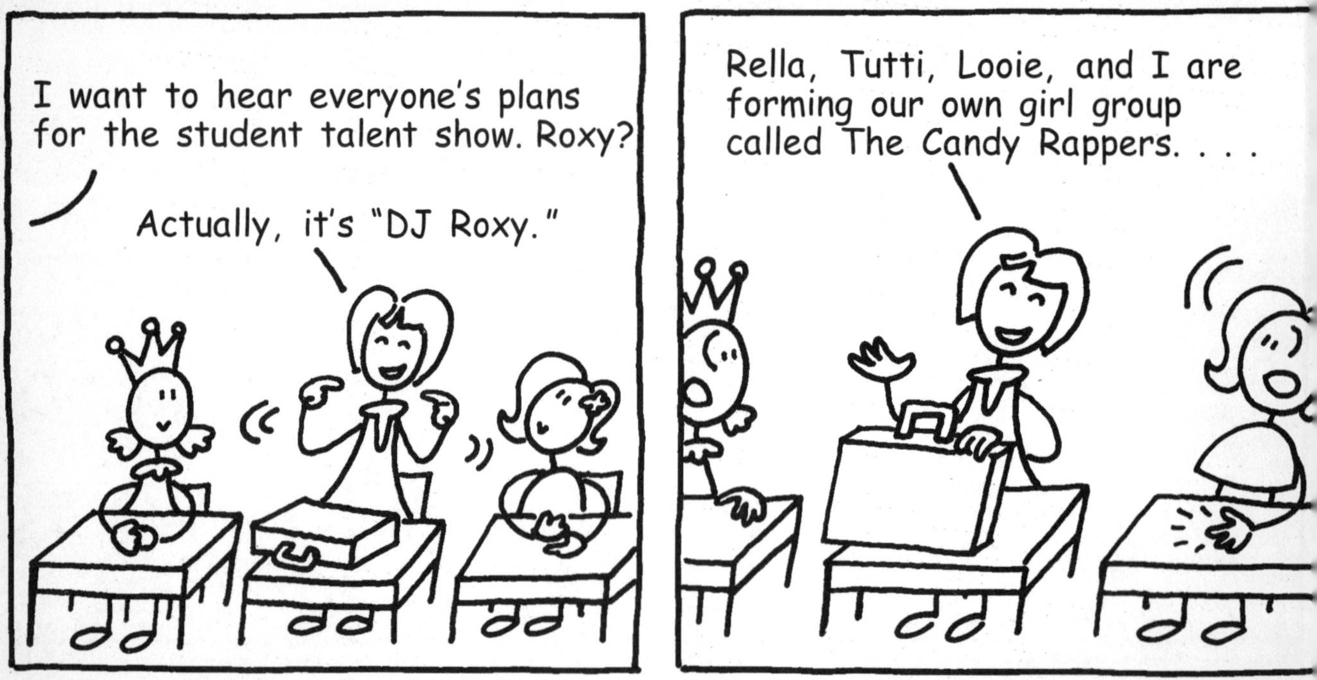
I want to hear everyone's plans for the student talent show. Roxy?
Actually, it's "DJ Roxy."
Rella, Tutti, Looie, and I are forming our own girl group called The Candy Rappers. . . .

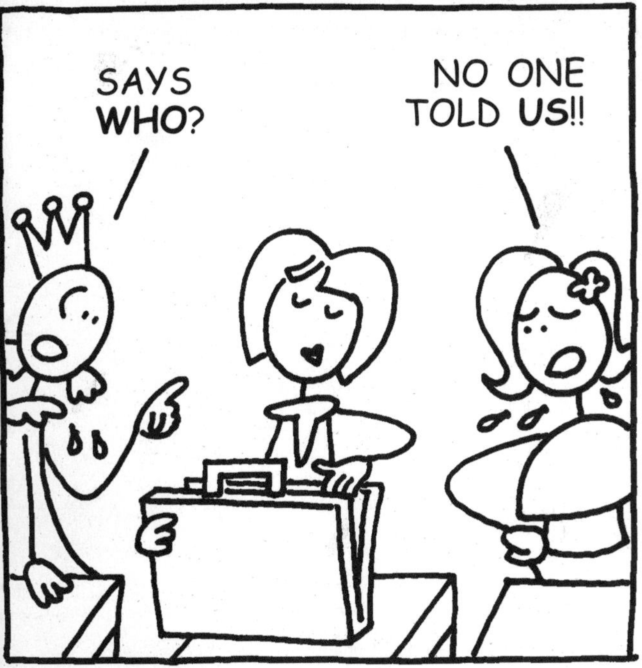
SAYS WHO?
NO ONE TOLD US!!

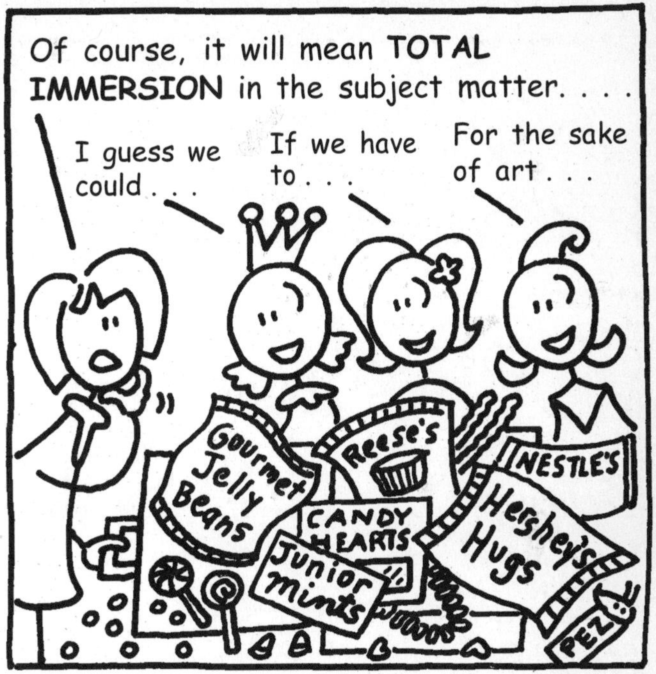
Of course, it will mean TOTAL IMMERSION in the subject matter. . . .
I guess we could . . .
If we have to . . .
For the sake of art . . .
Gourmet Jelly Beans
Reese's
NESTLE'S
CANDY HEARTS
Junior mints
Hershey's Hugs
PEZ

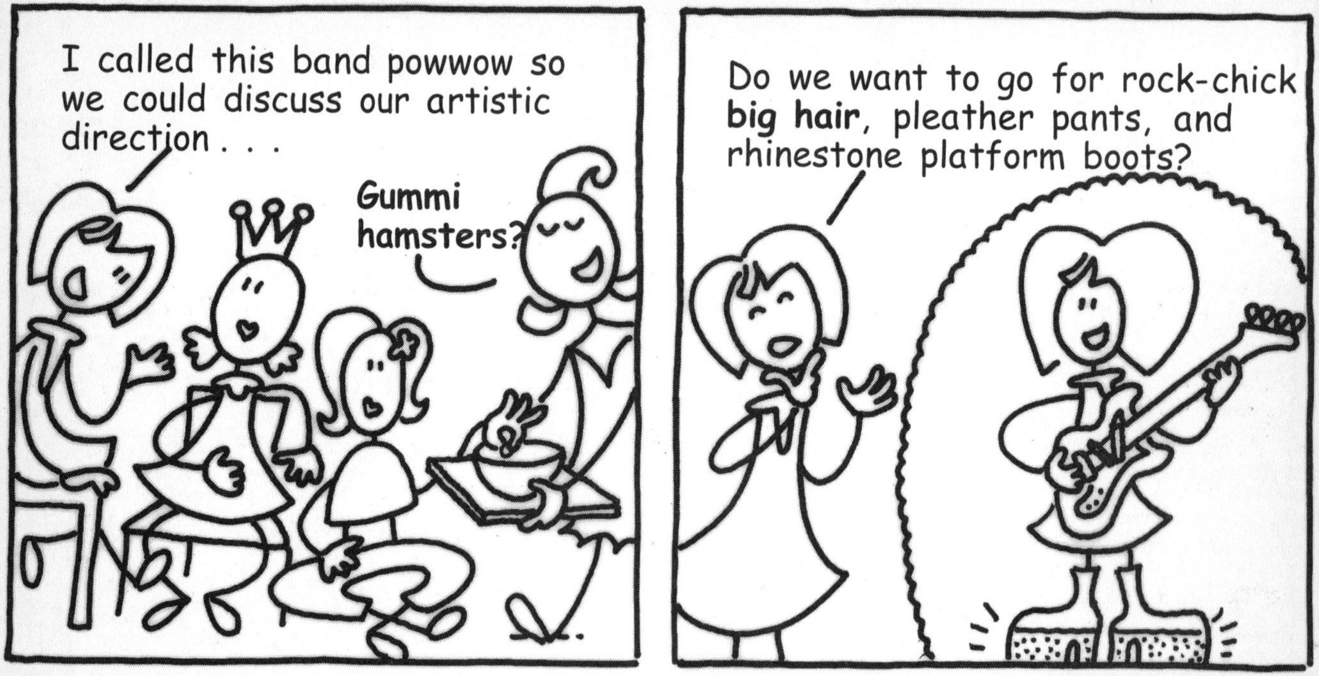
I called this band powwow so we could discuss our artistic direction . . .
Gummi hamsters?
Do we want to go for rock-chick **big hair**, pleather pants, and rhinestone platform boots?

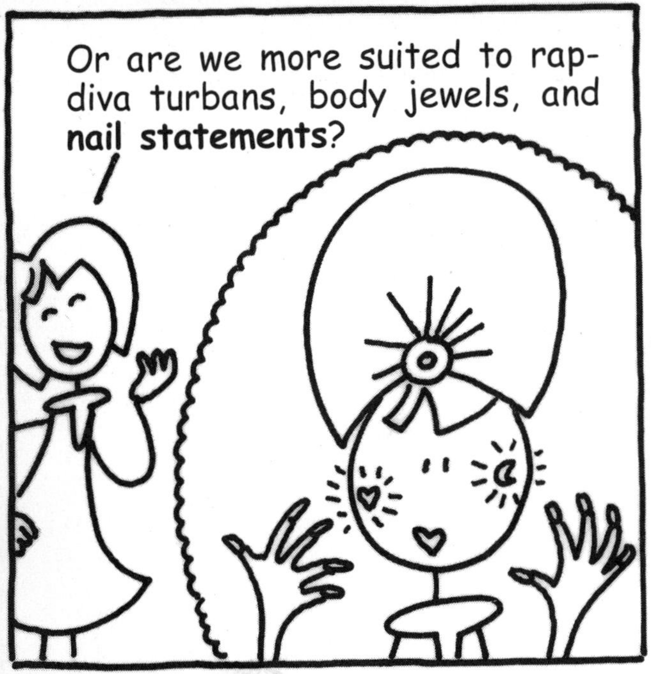
Or are we more suited to rap-diva turbans, body jewels, and **nail statements**?

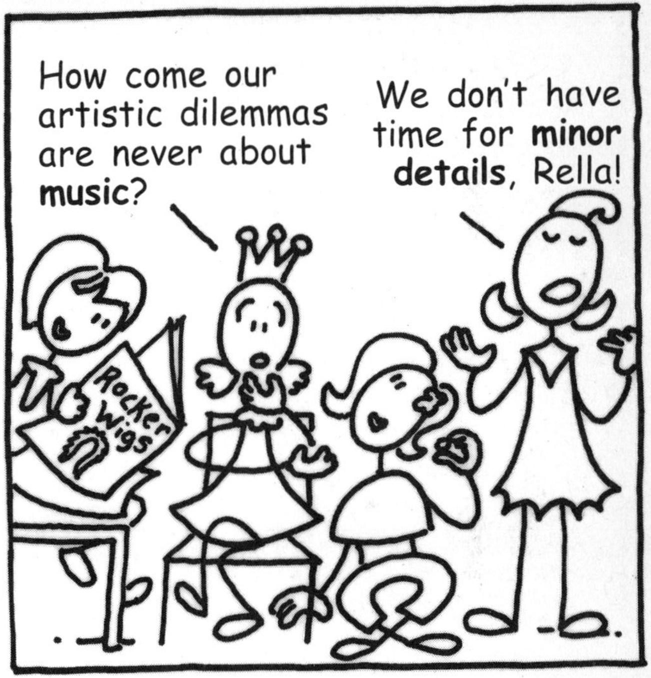
How come our artistic dilemmas are never about **music**?
We don't have time for **minor details**, Rella!
Rocker Wigs

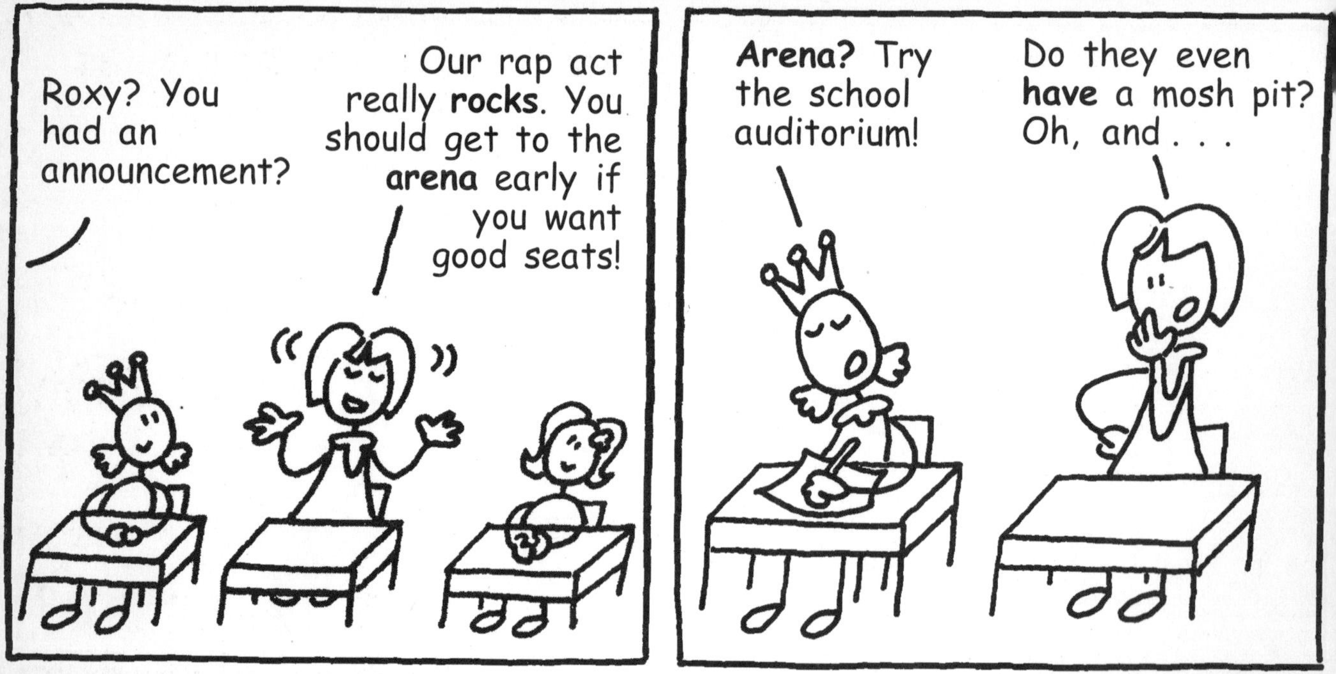
Roxy? You had an announcement?
Our rap act really **rocks**. You should get to the **arena** early if you want good seats!
Arena? Try the school auditorium!
Do they even **have** a mosh pit? Oh, and . . .

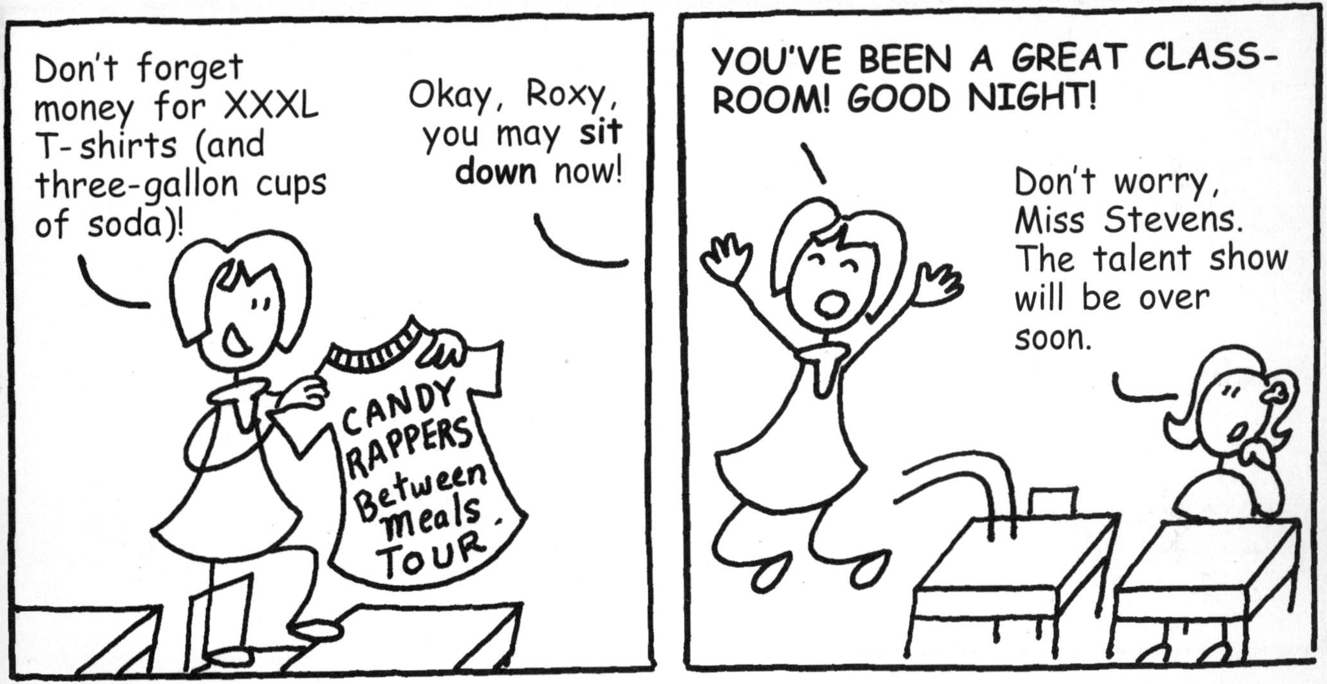
Don't forget money for XXXL T-shirts (and three-gallon cups of soda)!
CANDY RAPPERS Between Meals TOUR
Okay, Roxy, you may **sit down** now!
YOU'VE BEEN A GREAT CLASS-ROOM! GOOD NIGHT!
Don't worry, Miss Stevens. The talent show will be over soon.

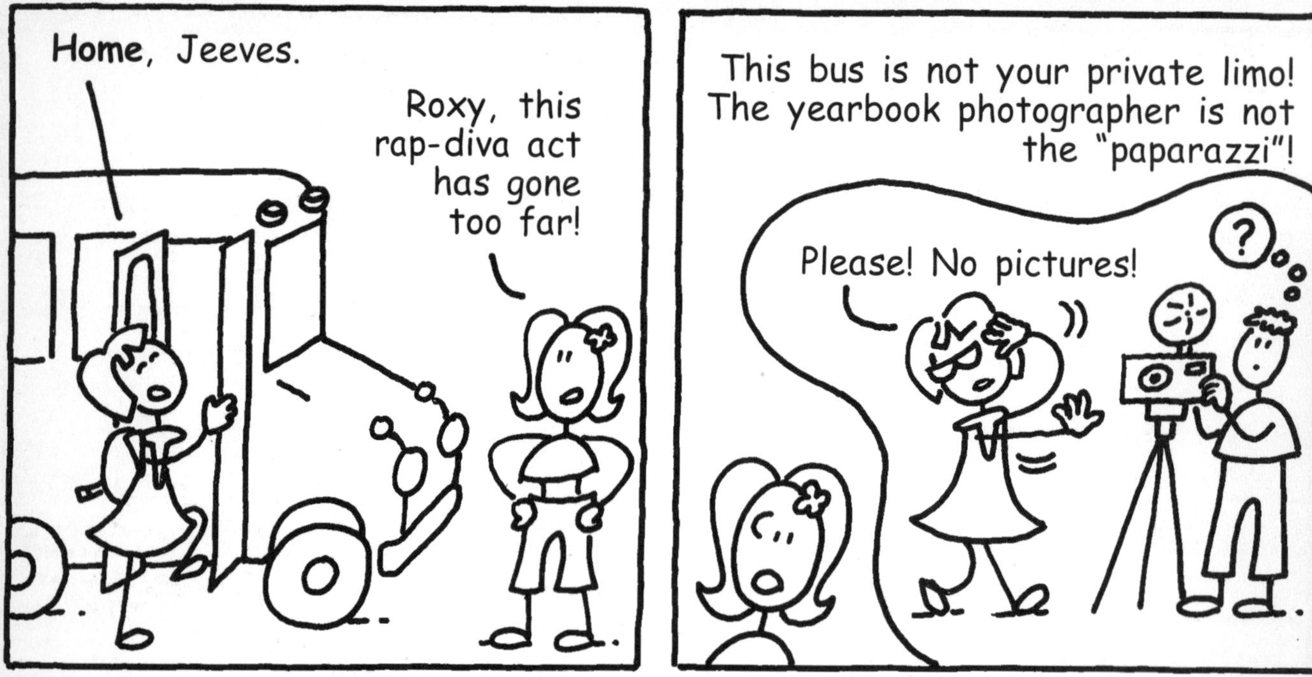
Home, Jeeves.
Roxy, this rap-diva act has gone too far!
This bus is not your private limo! The yearbook photographer is not the "paparazzi"!
Please! No pictures!
?

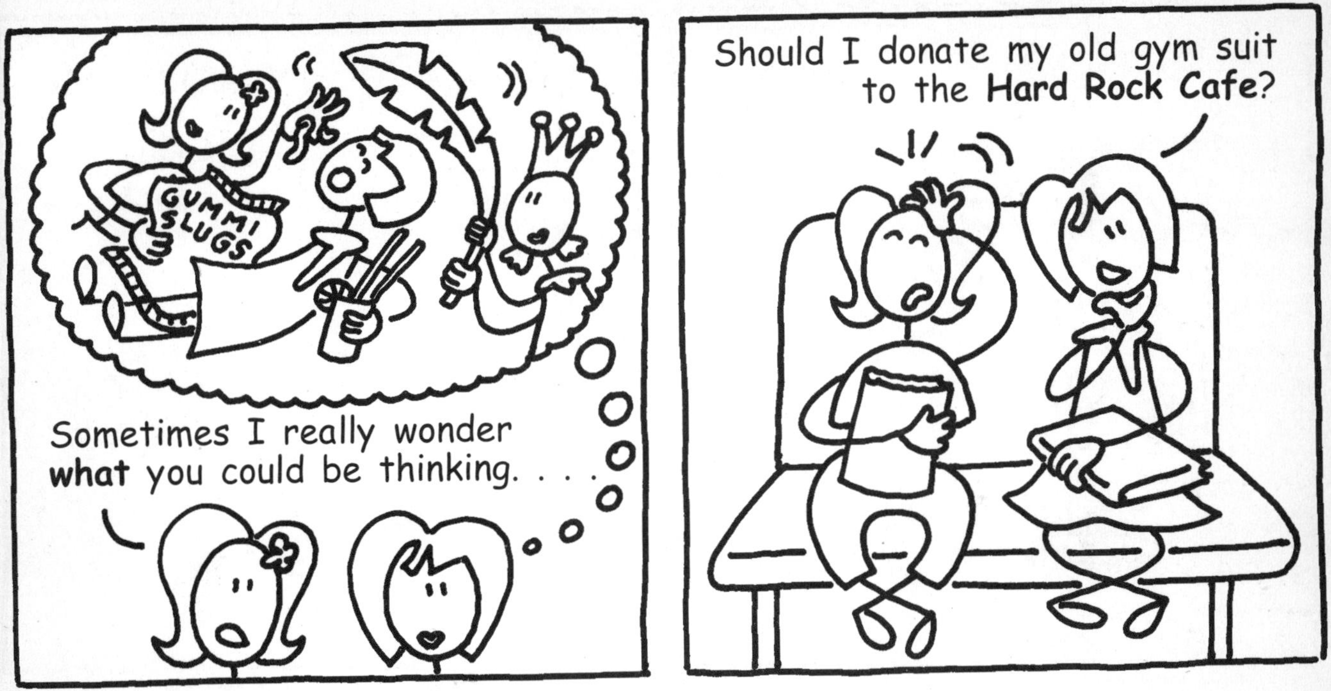
GUMMI SLUGS
Sometimes I really wonder **what** you could be thinking. . . .
Should I donate my old gym suit to the **Hard Rock Cafe**?

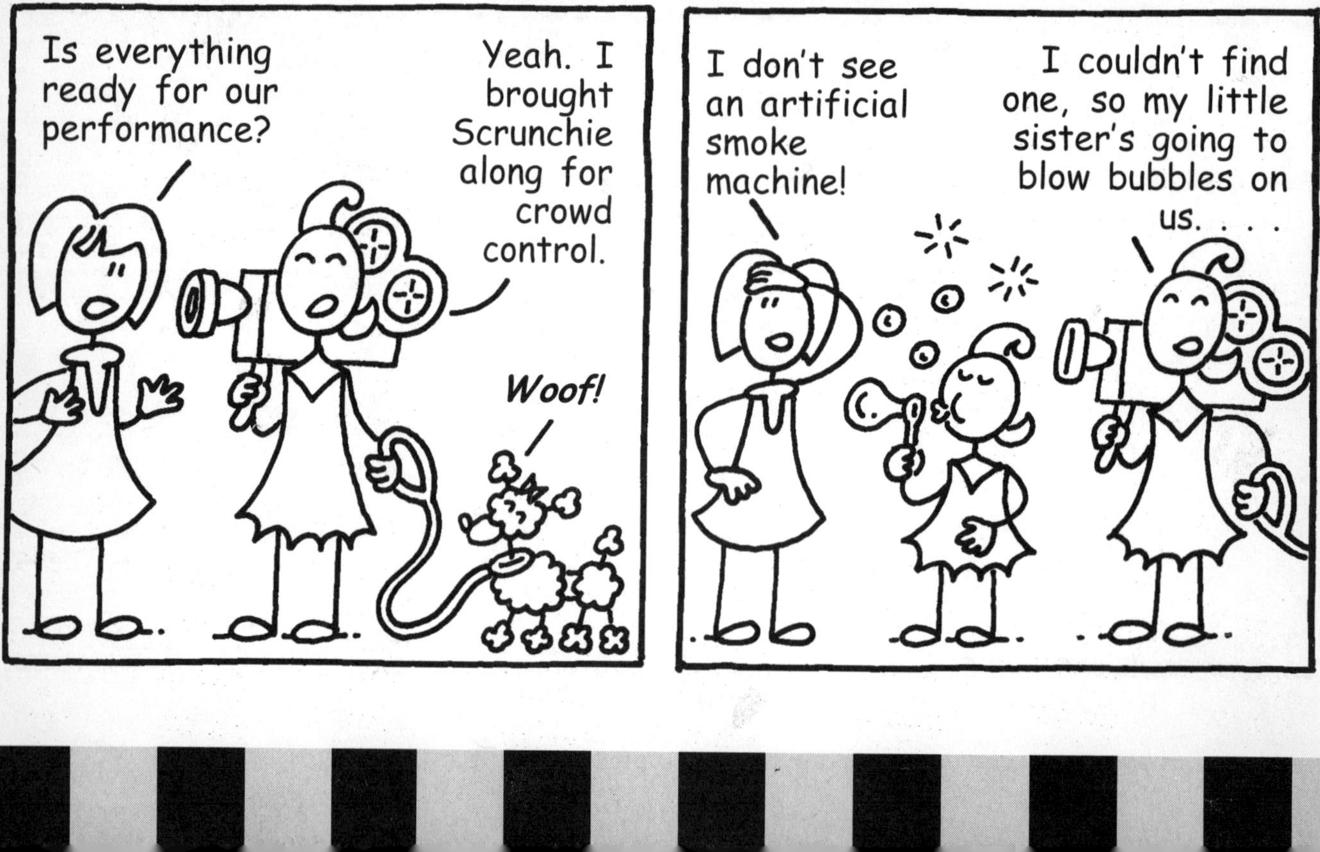
Is everything ready for our performance?
Yeah. I brought Scrunchie along for crowd control.
Woof!
I don't see an artificial smoke machine!
I couldn't find one, so my little sister's going to blow bubbles on us. . . .

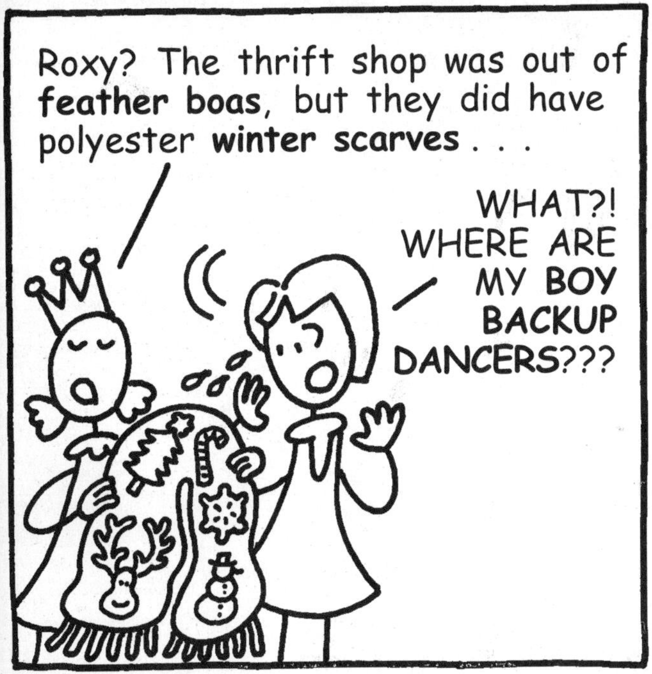
Roxy? The thrift shop was out of feather boas, but they did have polyester winter scarves . . .
WHAT?! WHERE ARE MY BOY BACKUP DANCERS???

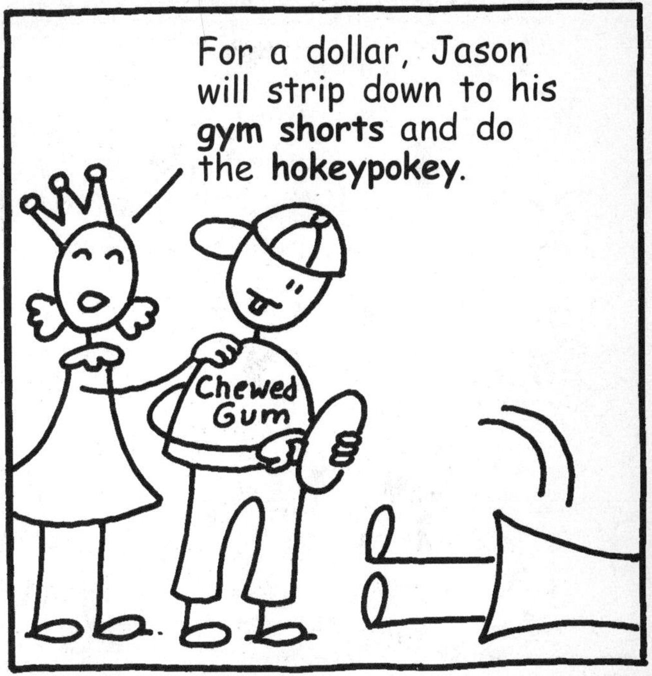
For a dollar, Jason will strip down to his gym shorts and do the hokeypokey.
Chewed Gum

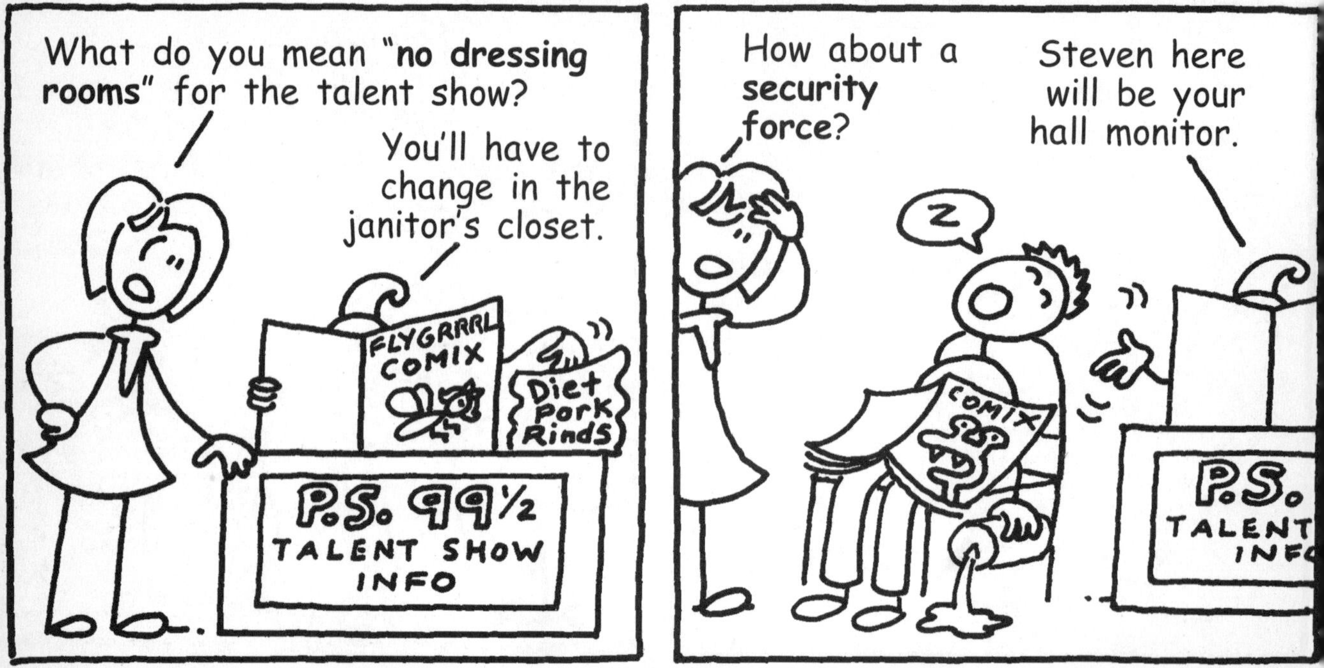
What do you mean "**no dressing rooms**" for the talent show?
You'll have to change in the janitor's closet.
FLYGRRRL COMIX
Diet Pork Rinds
P.S. 99½ TALENT SHOW INFO
How about a **security force**?
Z
COMIX
Steven here will be your hall monitor.
P.S. TALENT INFO

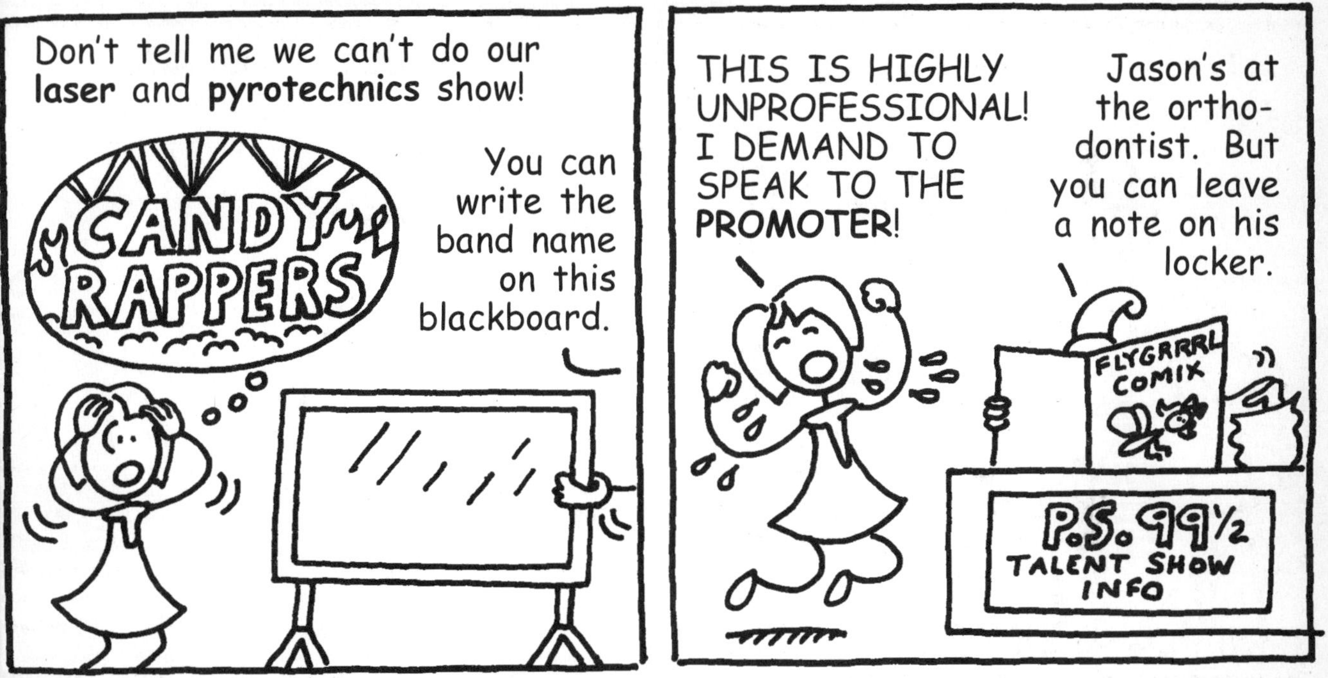
Don't tell me we can't do our **laser** and **pyrotechnics** show!
CANDY RAPPERS
You can write the band name on this blackboard.
THIS IS HIGHLY UNPROFESSIONAL! I DEMAND TO SPEAK TO THE **PROMOTER**!
Jason's at the orthodontist. But you can leave a note on his locker.
FLYGRRRL COMIX
P.S. 99½
TALENT SHOW INFO

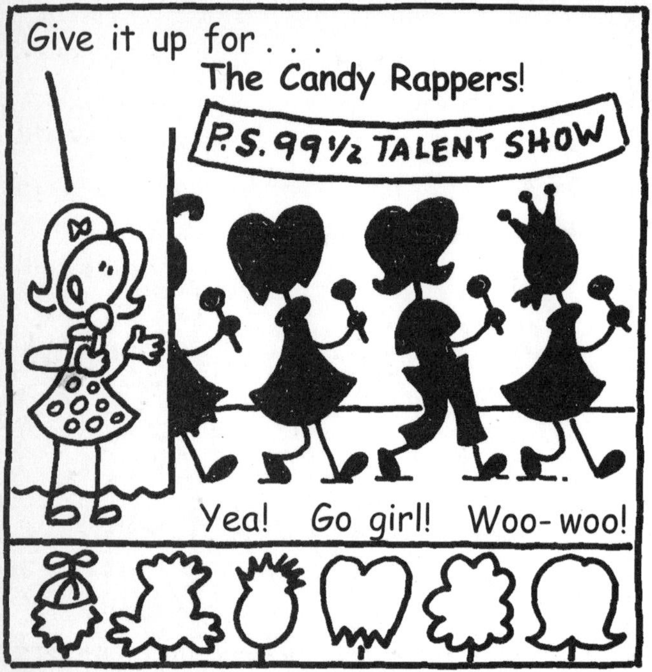
Give it up for . . .
The Candy Rappers!
P.S. 99½ TALENT SHOW
Yea!
Go girl!
Woo-woo!

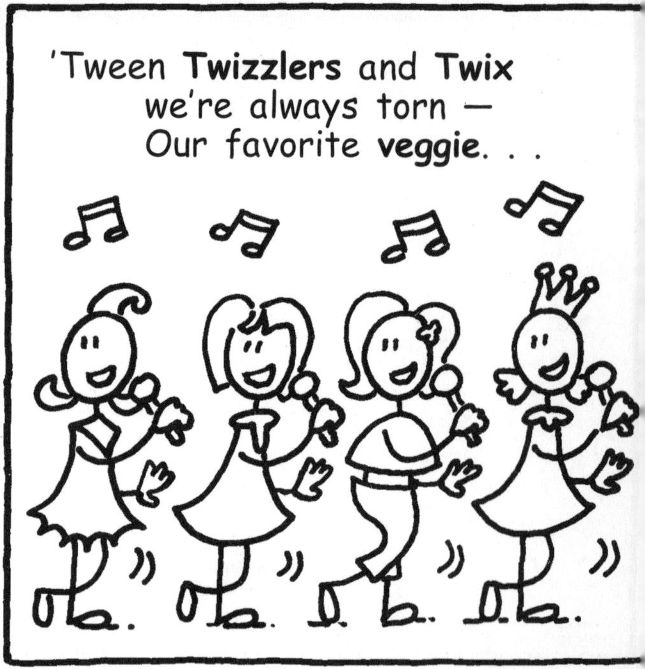
'Tween Twizzlers and Twix
we're always torn —
Our favorite veggie. . .

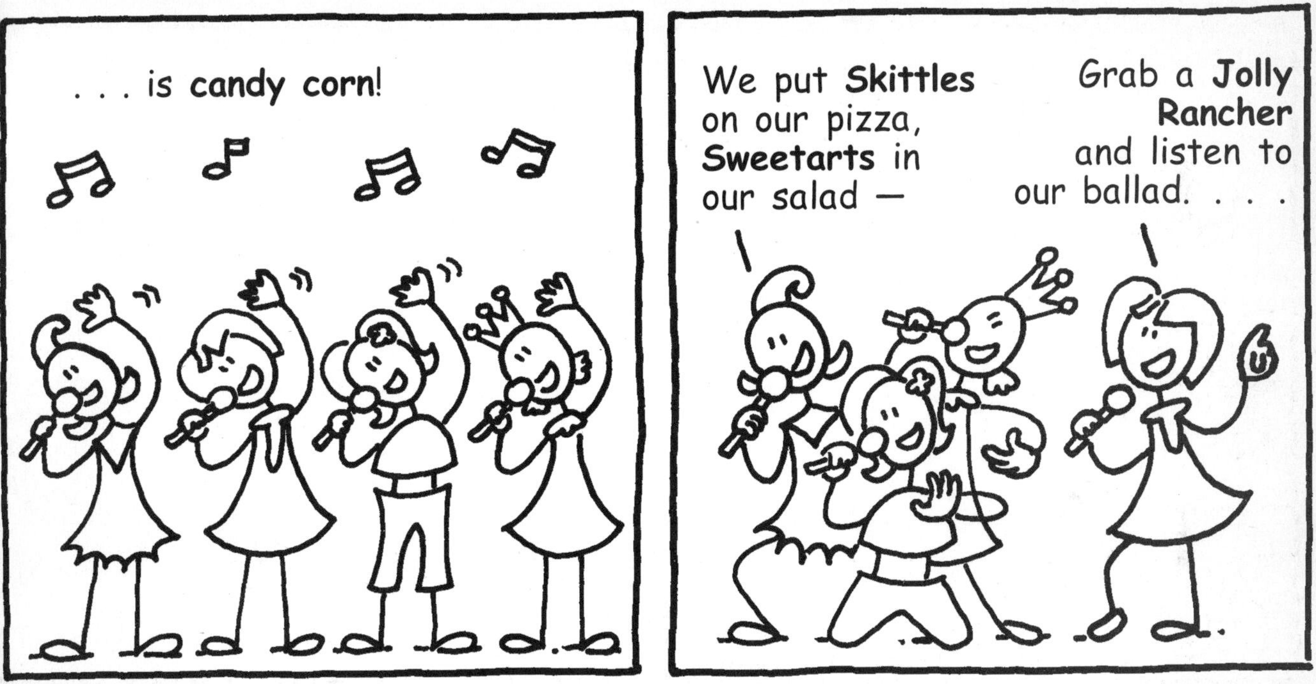
. . . is candy corn!
We put Skittles on our pizza, Sweetarts in our salad —
Grab a Jolly Rancher and listen to our ballad. . . .

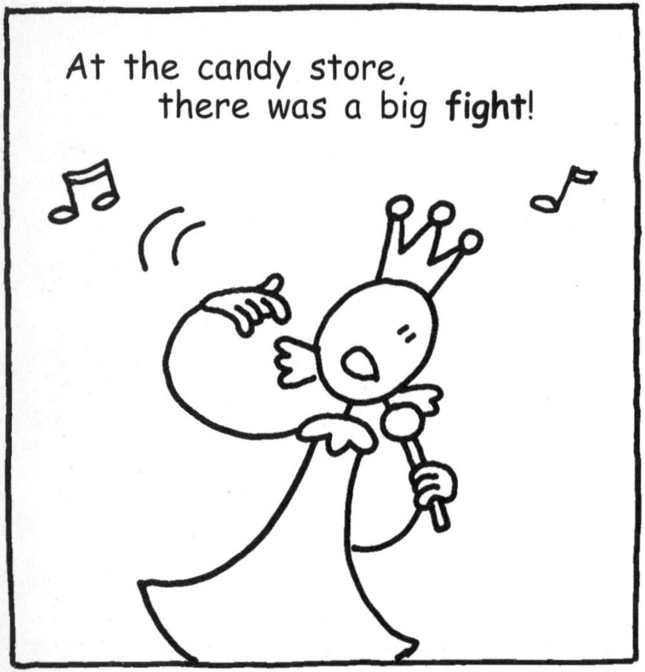
At the candy store,
there was a big **fight**!

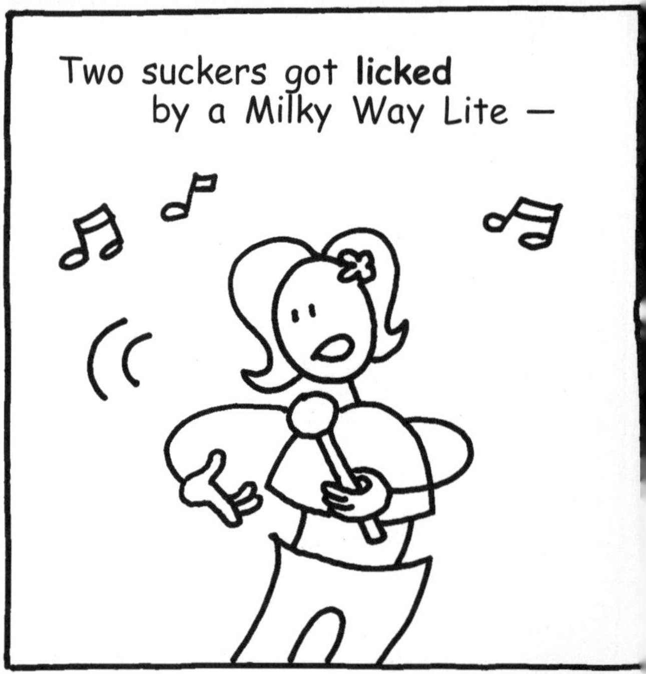
Two suckers got **licked**
by a Milky Way Lite —

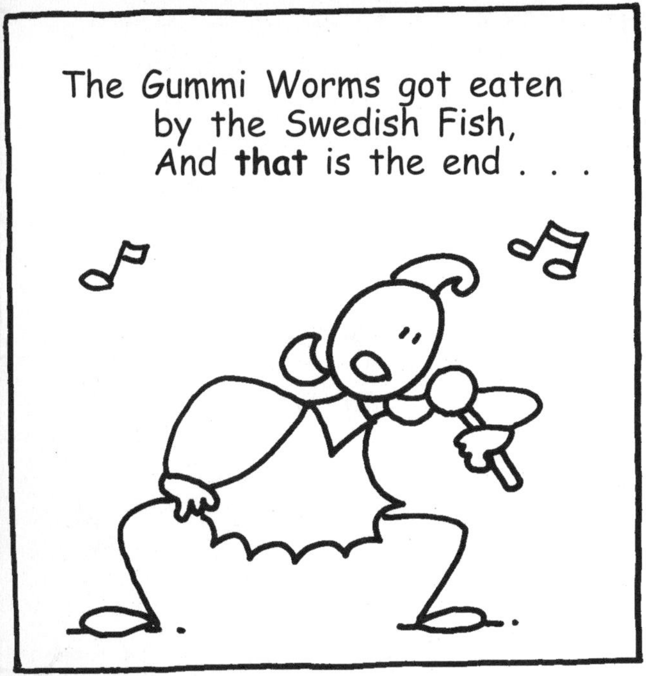
The Gummi Worms got eaten
by the Swedish Fish,
And **that** is the end . . .

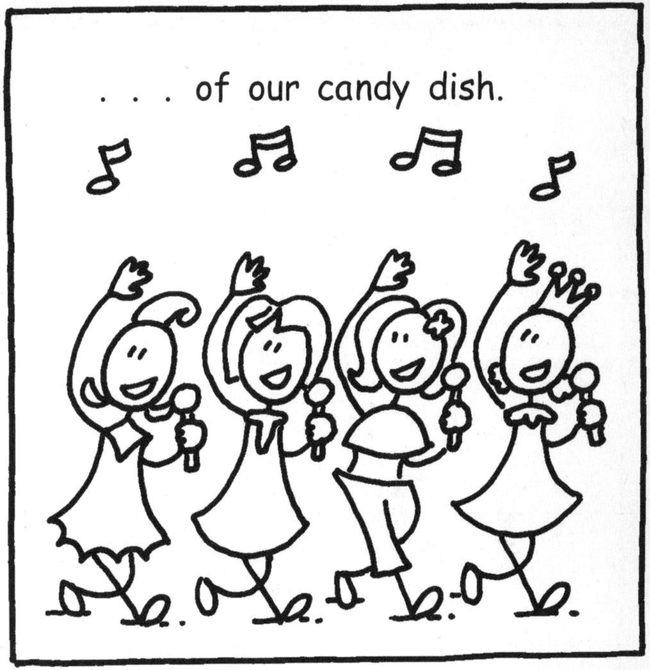
. . . of our candy dish.

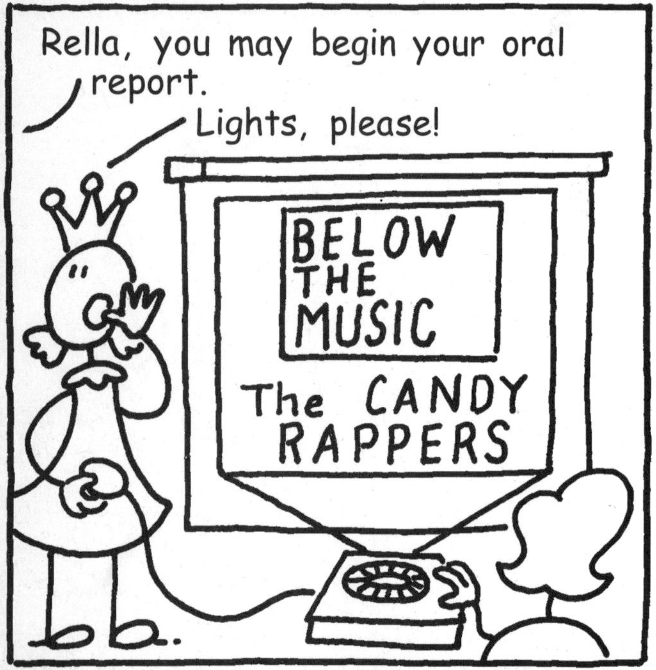
Rella, you may begin your oral report.
Lights, please!
BELOW THE MUSIC
The CANDY RAPPERS

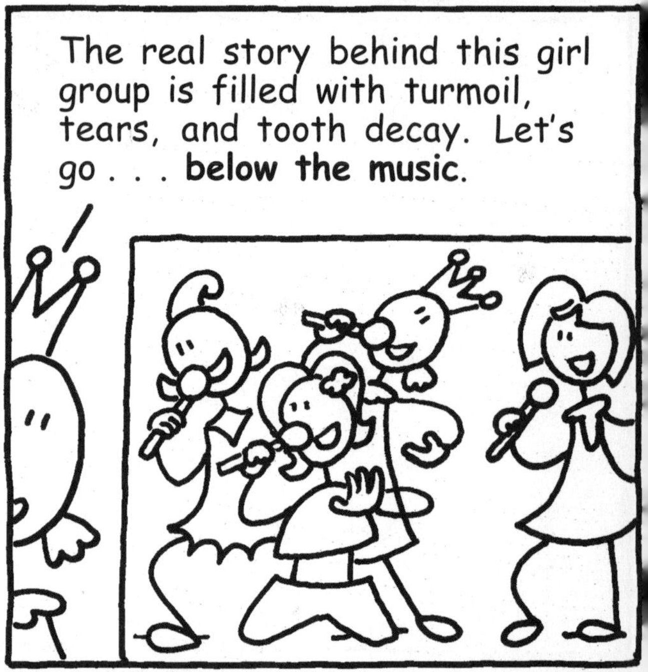
The real story behind this girl group is filled with turmoil, tears, and tooth decay. Let's go . . . **below the music**.

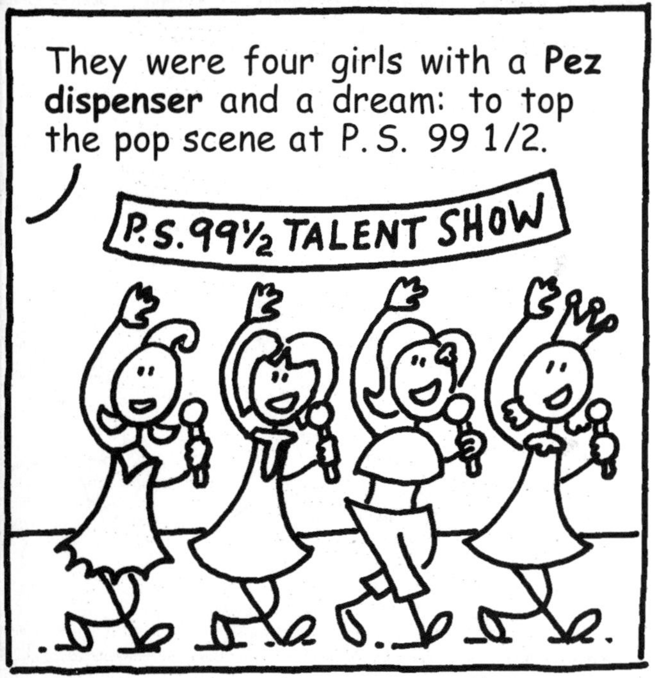
They were four girls with a **Pez dispenser** and a dream: to top the pop scene at P. S. 99 1/2.
P.S. 99½ TALENT SHOW

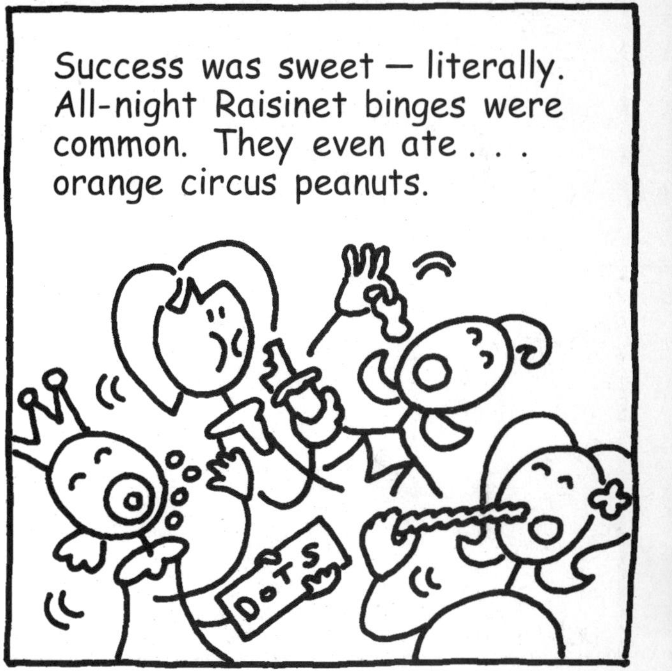
Success was sweet — literally. All-night Raisinet binges were common. They even ate . . . orange circus peanuts.
DOTS

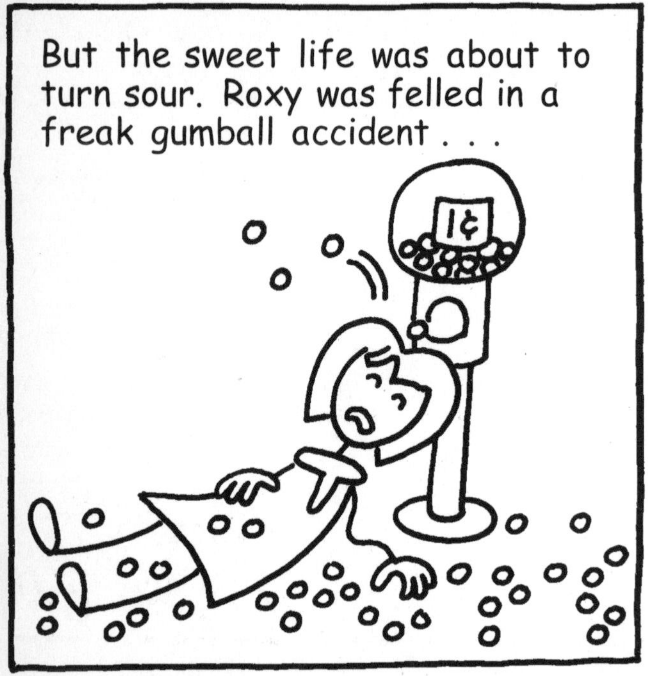
But the sweet life was about to turn sour. Roxy was felled in a freak gumball accident . . .
1¢

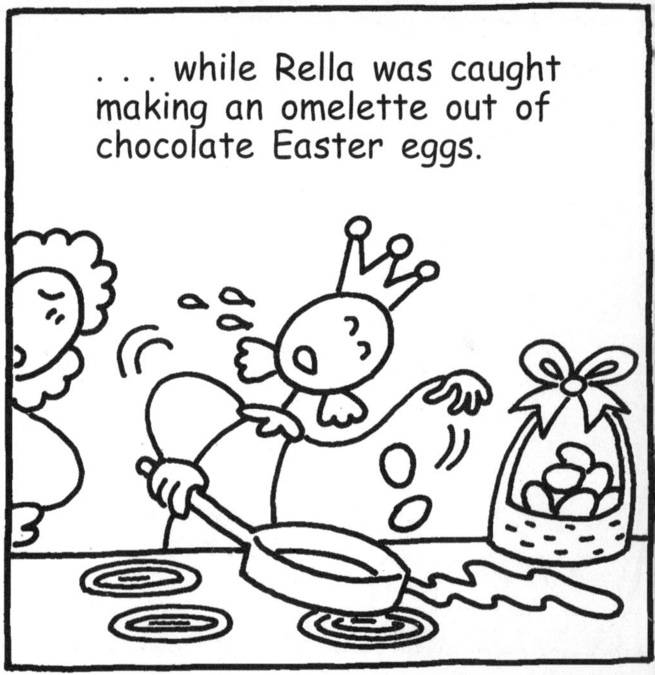
. . . while Rella was caught making an omelette out of chocolate Easter eggs.

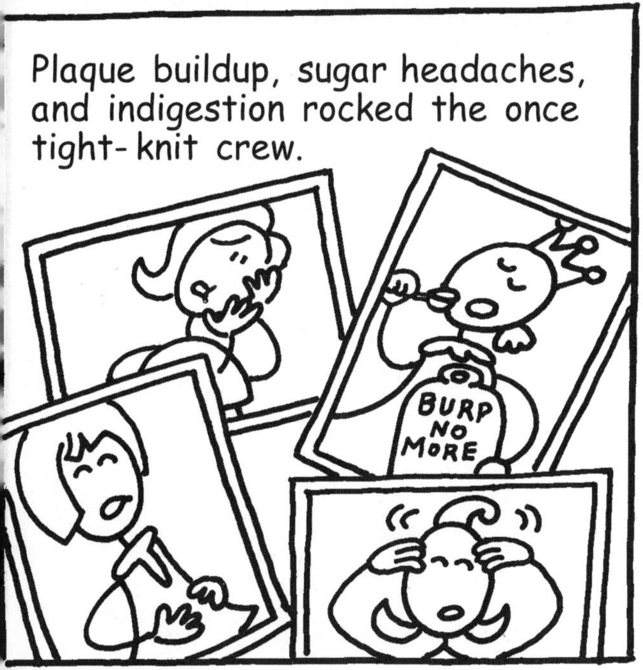
Plaque buildup, sugar headaches, and indigestion rocked the once tight-knit crew.
BURP NO MORE

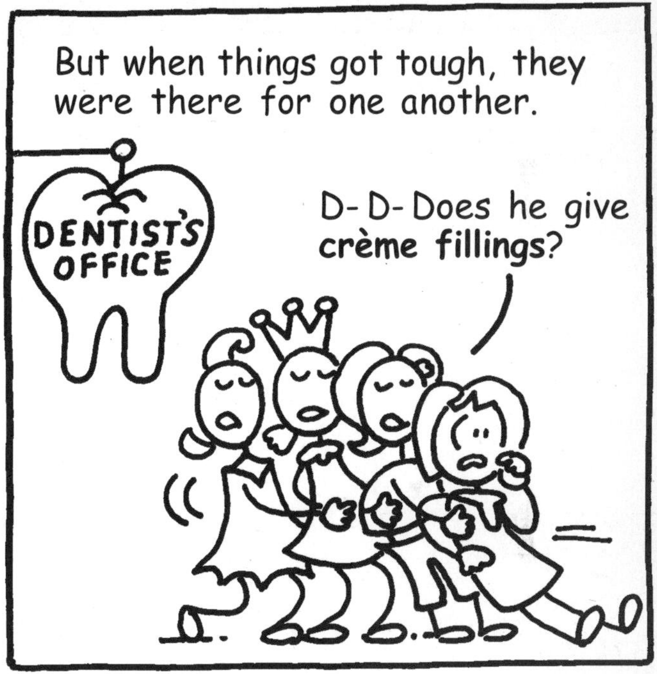
But when things got tough, they were there for one another.
DENTIST'S OFFICE
D-D-Does he give **crème** fillings?

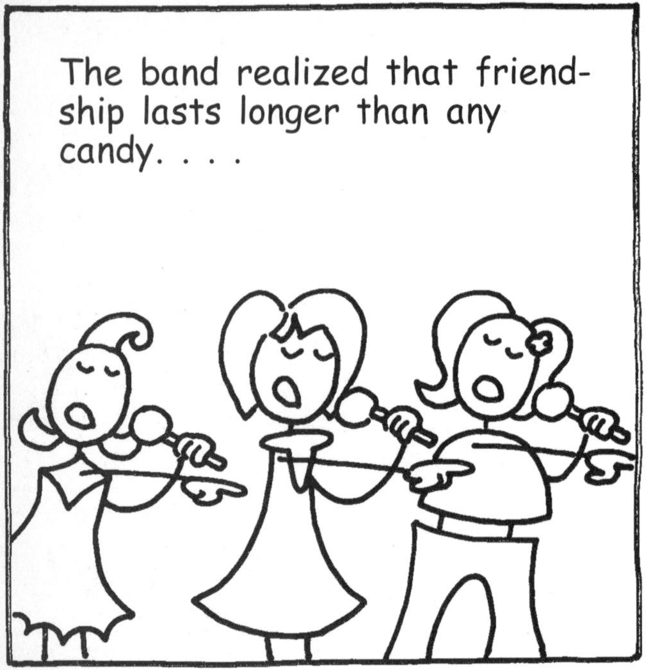
The band realized that friend-ship lasts longer than any candy. . . .

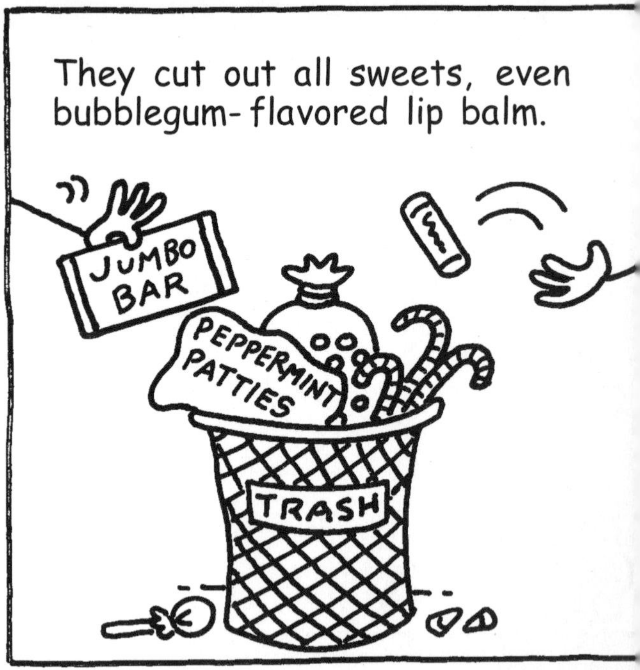
They cut out all sweets, even bubblegum-flavored lip balm.
JUMBO BAR
PEPPERMINT PATTIES
TRASH

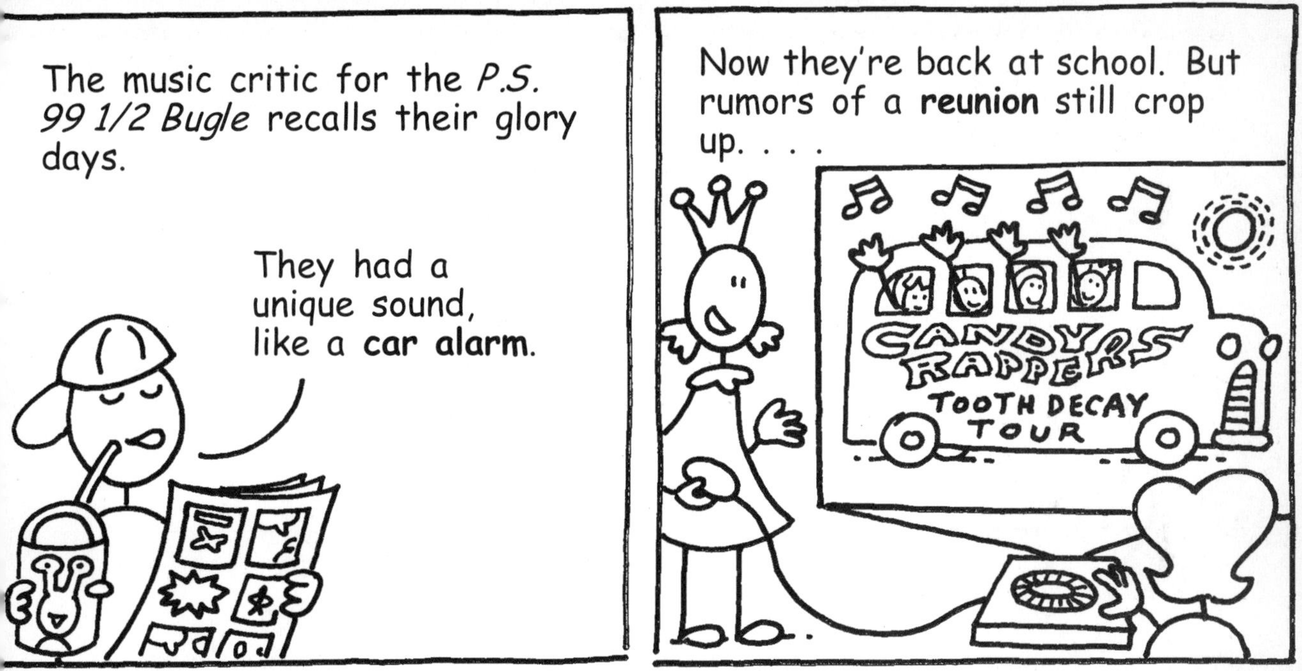
The music critic for the *P.S. 99 1/2 Bugle* recalls their glory days.
They had a unique sound, like a **car alarm**.
Now they're back at school. But rumors of a **reunion** still crop up. . . .
CANDY WRAPPERS
TOOTH DECAY TOUR

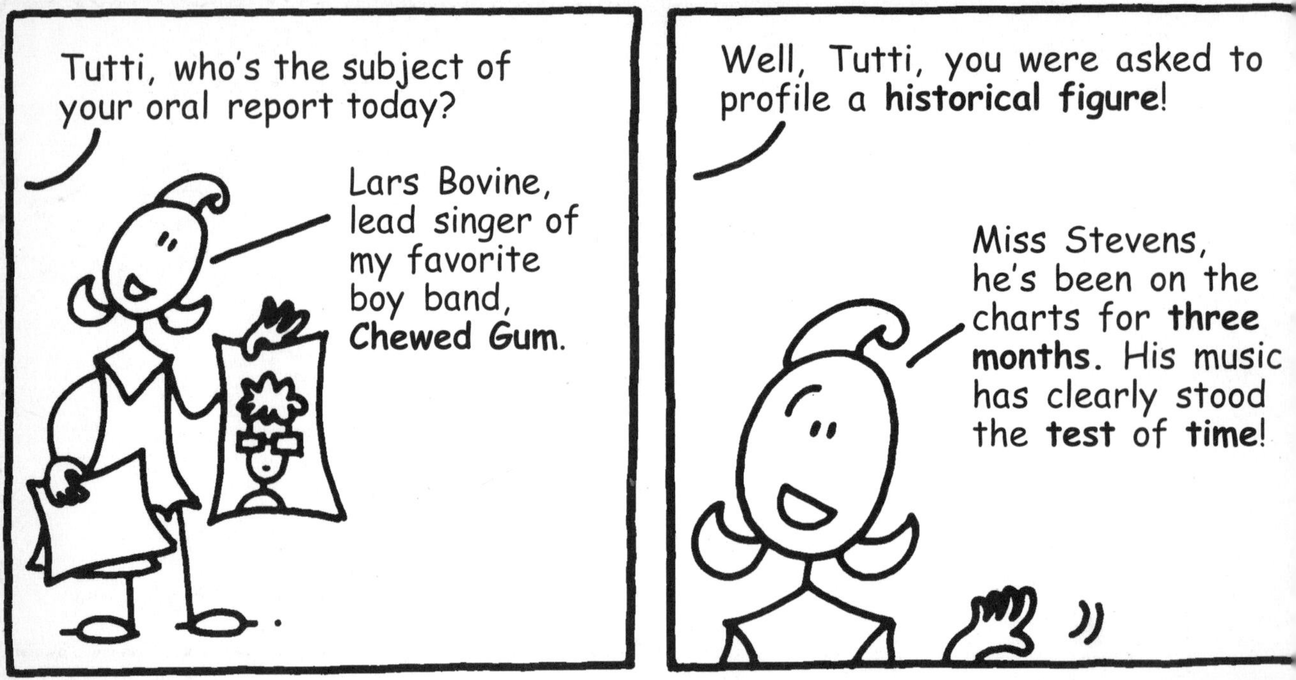
Tutti, who's the subject of your oral report today?
Lars Bovine, lead singer of my favorite boy band, **Chewed Gum**.
Well, Tutti, you were asked to profile a **historical figure**!
Miss Stevens, he's been on the charts for **three months.** His music has clearly stood the **test** of **time**!

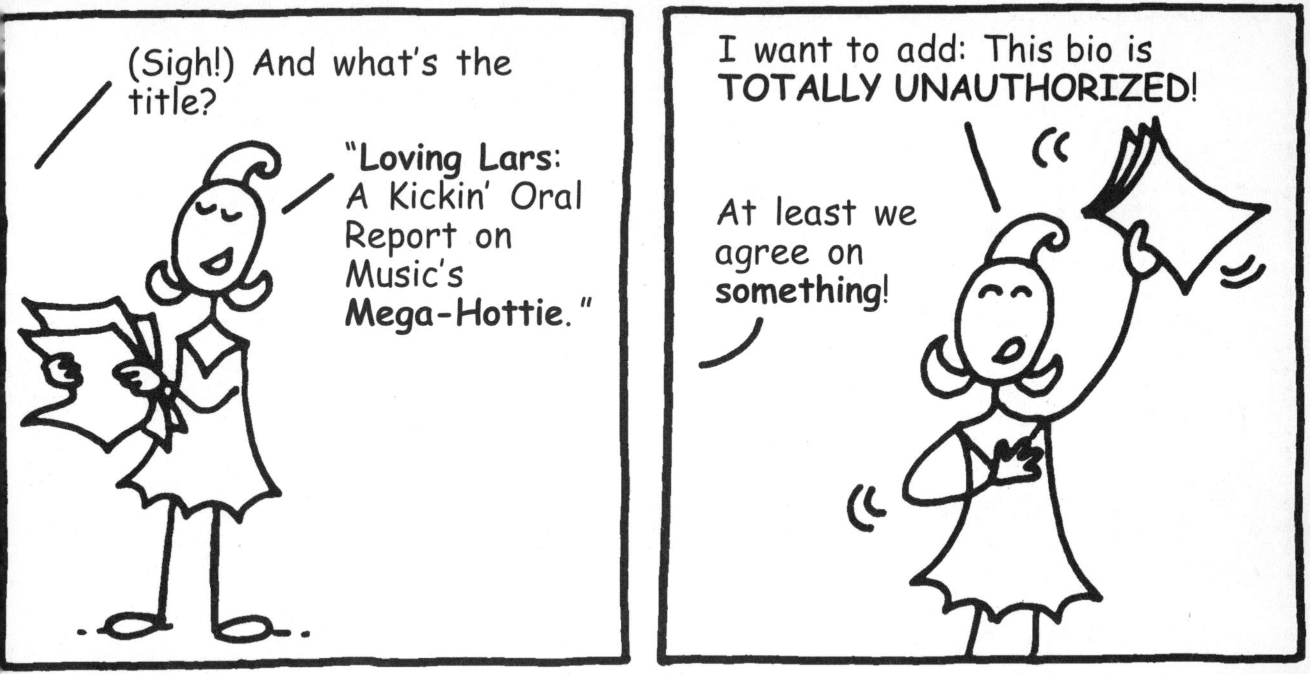
(Sigh!) And what's the title?
"**Loving Lars**: A Kickin' Oral Report on Music's **Mega-Hottie**."
I want to add: This bio is **TOTALLY UNAUTHORIZED**!
At least we agree on **something**!

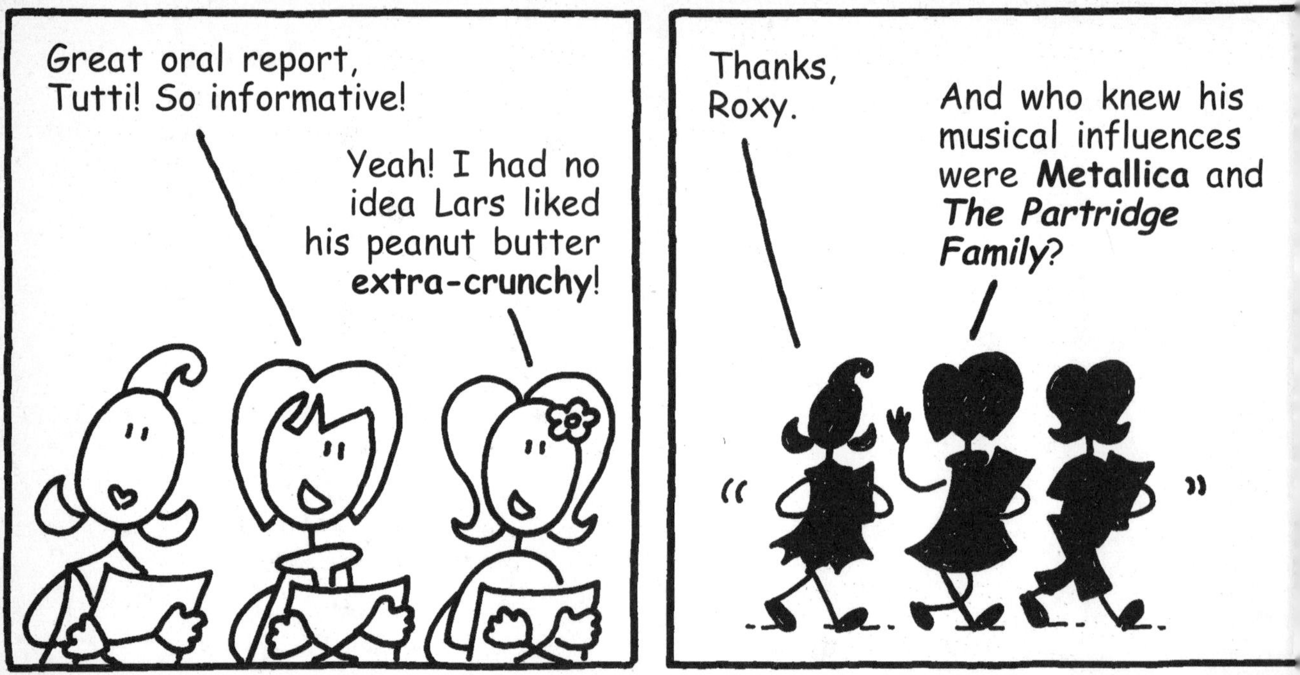
Great oral report, Tutti! So informative!
Yeah! I had no idea Lars liked his peanut butter **extra-crunchy**!
Thanks, Roxy.
And who knew his musical influences were **Metallica** and ***The Partridge Family***?

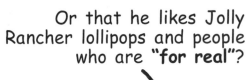

Or that he likes Jolly Rancher lollipops and people who are **"for real"**?

Even Miss Stevens kept saying **"I can't believe it."**

I guess she didn't realize Lars was an **innie!**

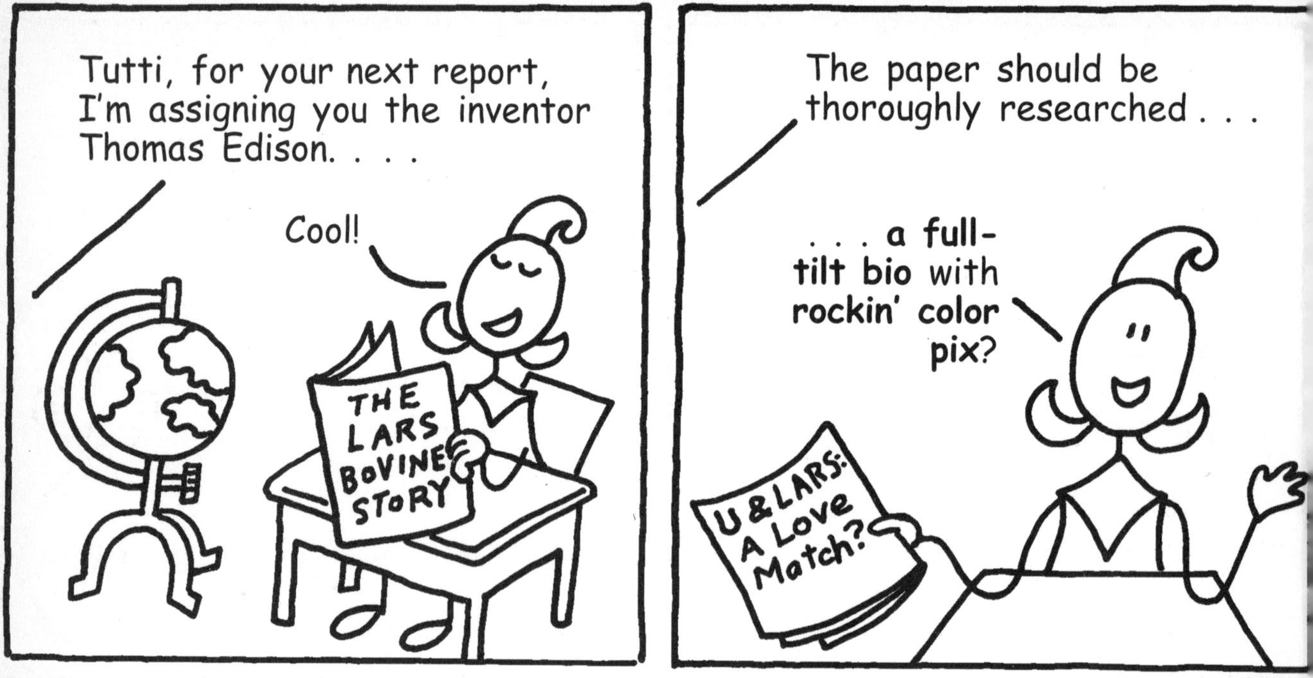

Tutti, for your next report, I'm assigning you the inventor Thomas Edison. . . .
Cool!
THE LARS BoVINE STORY
The paper should be thoroughly researched . . .
. . . a full-tilt bio with rockin' color pix?
U & LARS: A Love Match?

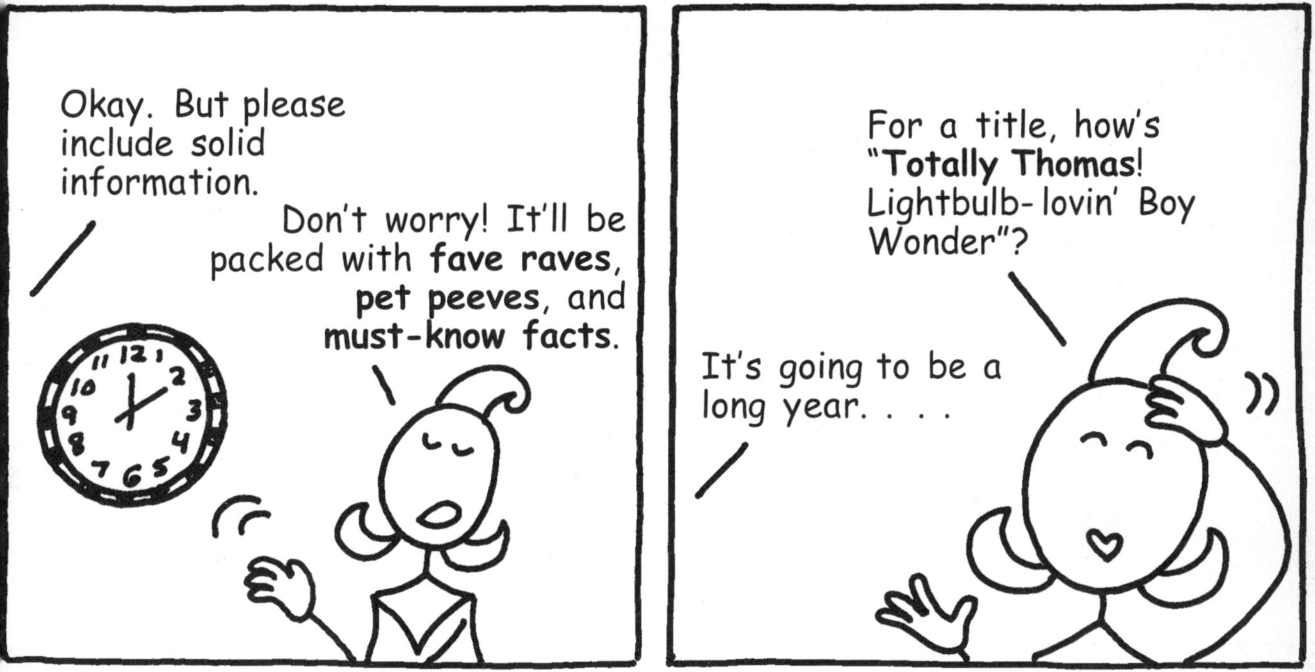
Okay. But please include solid information.
Don't worry! It'll be packed with **fave raves**, **pet peeves**, and **must-know facts**.
For a title, how's "**Totally Thomas**! Lightbulb-lovin' Boy Wonder"?
It's going to be a long year. . . .

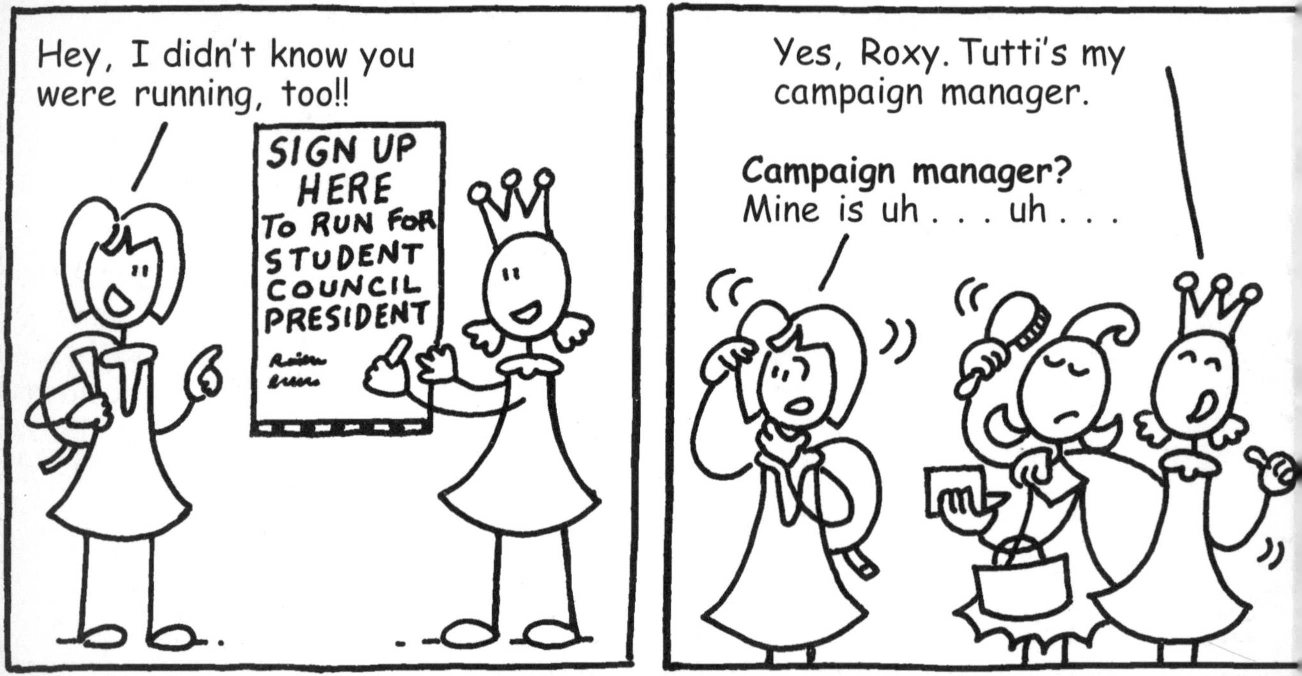
Hey, I didn't know you were running, too!!
SIGN UP HERE TO RUN FOR STUDENT COUNCIL PRESIDENT
Yes, Roxy. Tutti's my campaign manager.
Campaign manager? Mine is uh . . . uh . . .

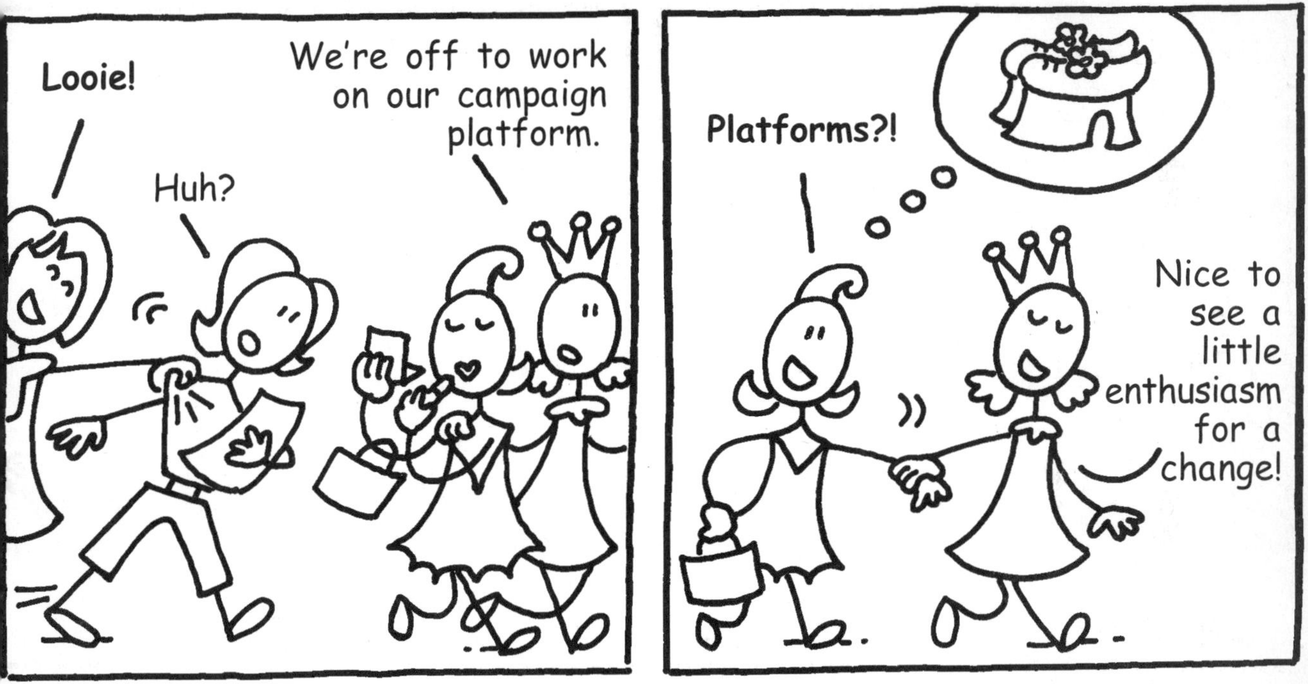
Looie!
Huh?
We're off to work on our campaign platform.
Platforms?!
Nice to see a little enthusiasm for a change!

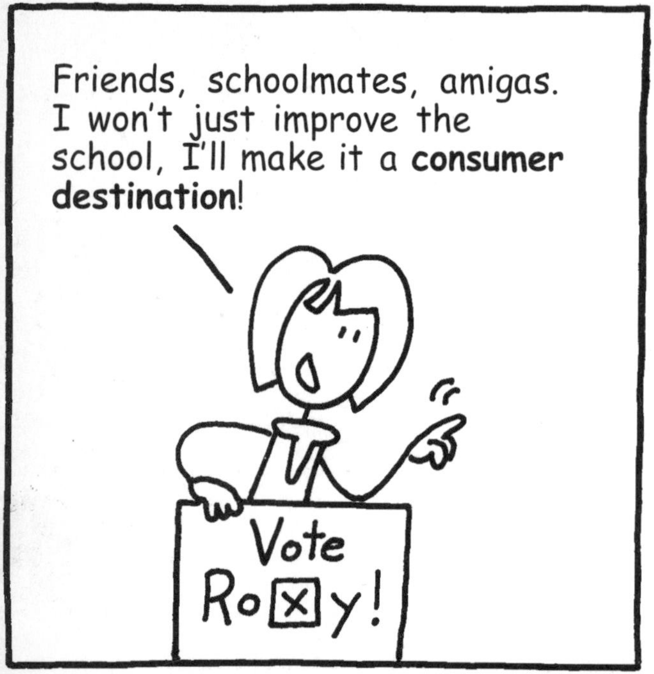
Friends, schoolmates, amigas. I won't just improve the school, I'll make it a **consumer destination**!
Vote Roxy!

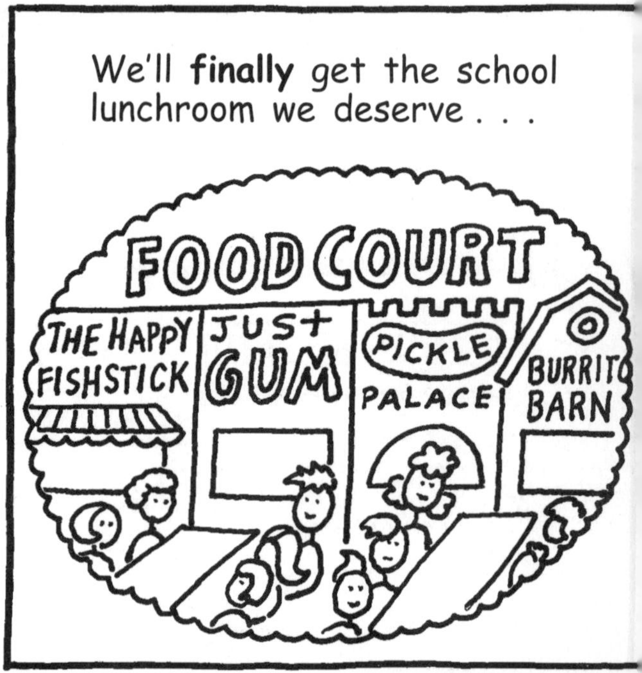
We'll **finally** get the school lunchroom we deserve . . .
FOOD COURT
THE HAPPY FISHSTICK
JUST GUM
PICKLE PALACE
BURRITO BARN

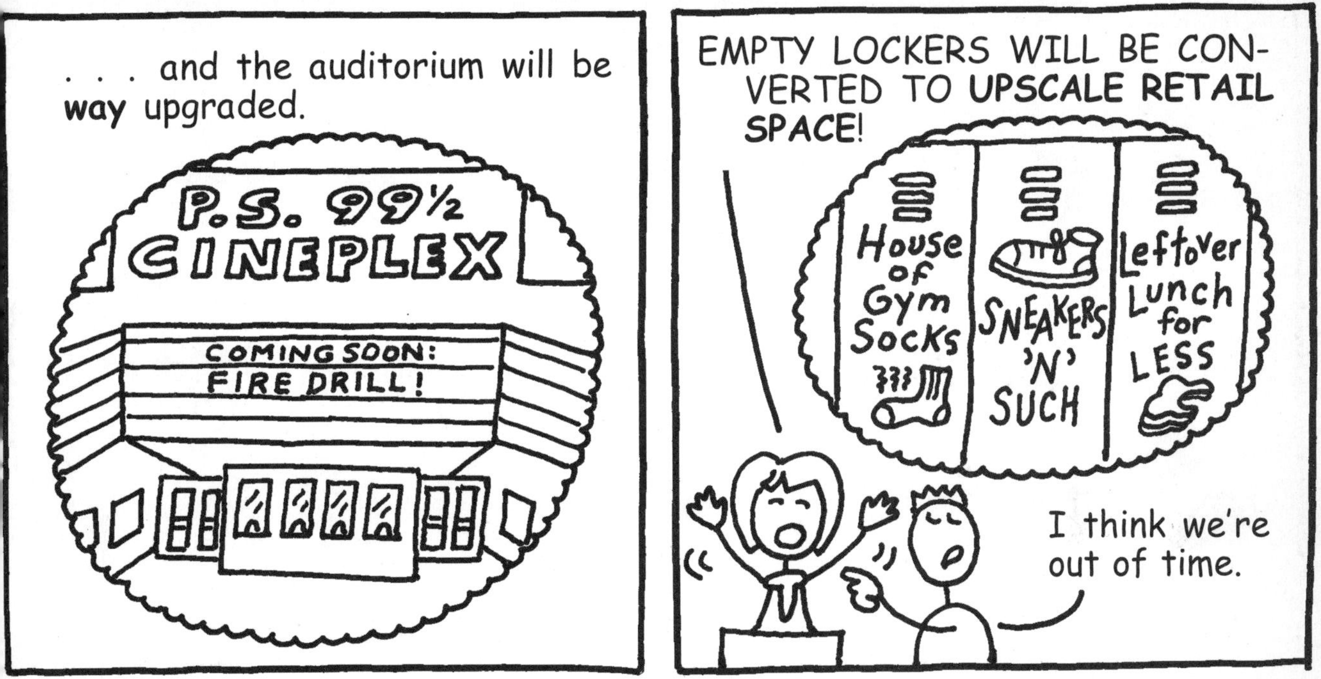
. . . and the auditorium will be **way** upgraded.
P.S. 99½
CINEPLEX
COMING SOON:
FIRE DRILL!
EMPTY LOCKERS WILL BE CONVERTED TO **UPSCALE RETAIL SPACE!**
House of Gym Socks
SNEAKERS 'N' SUCH
Leftover Lunch for LESS
I think we're out of time.

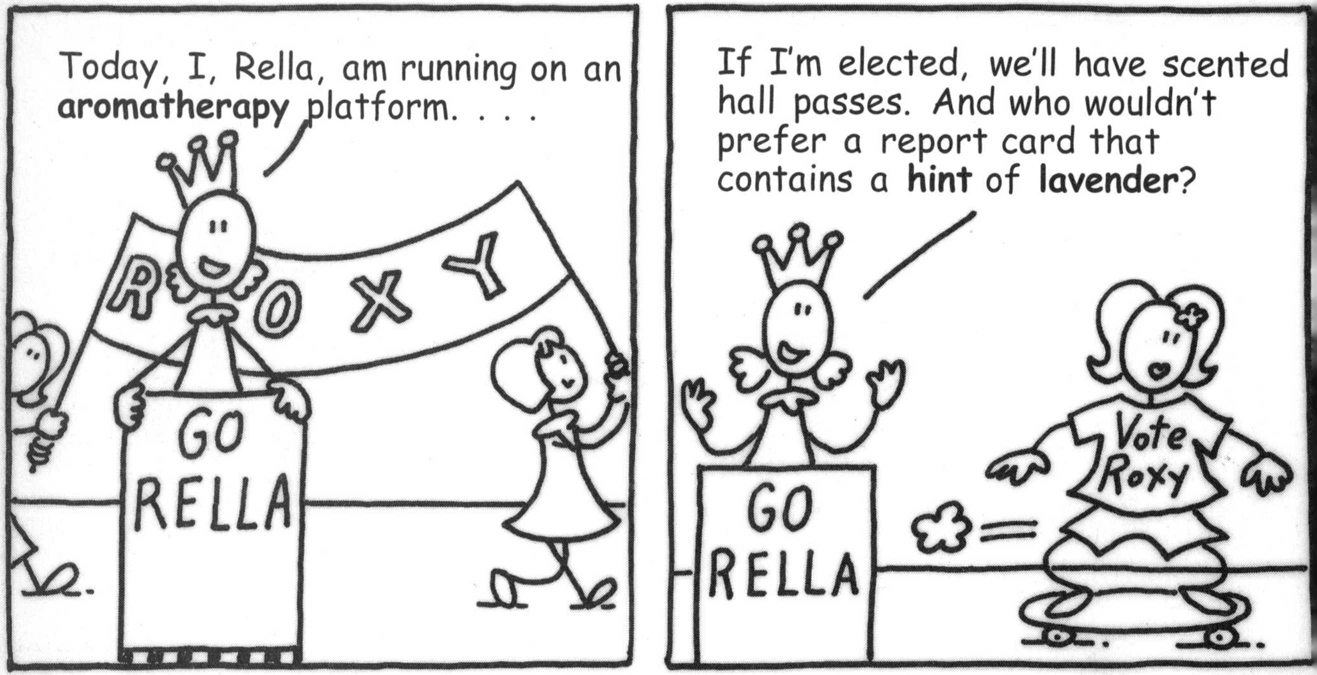
Today, I, Rella, am running on an **aromatherapy** platform. . . .
ROXY
GO RELLA
If I'm elected, we'll have scented hall passes. And who wouldn't prefer a report card that contains a **hint** of **lavender**?
GO RELLA
Vote Roxy

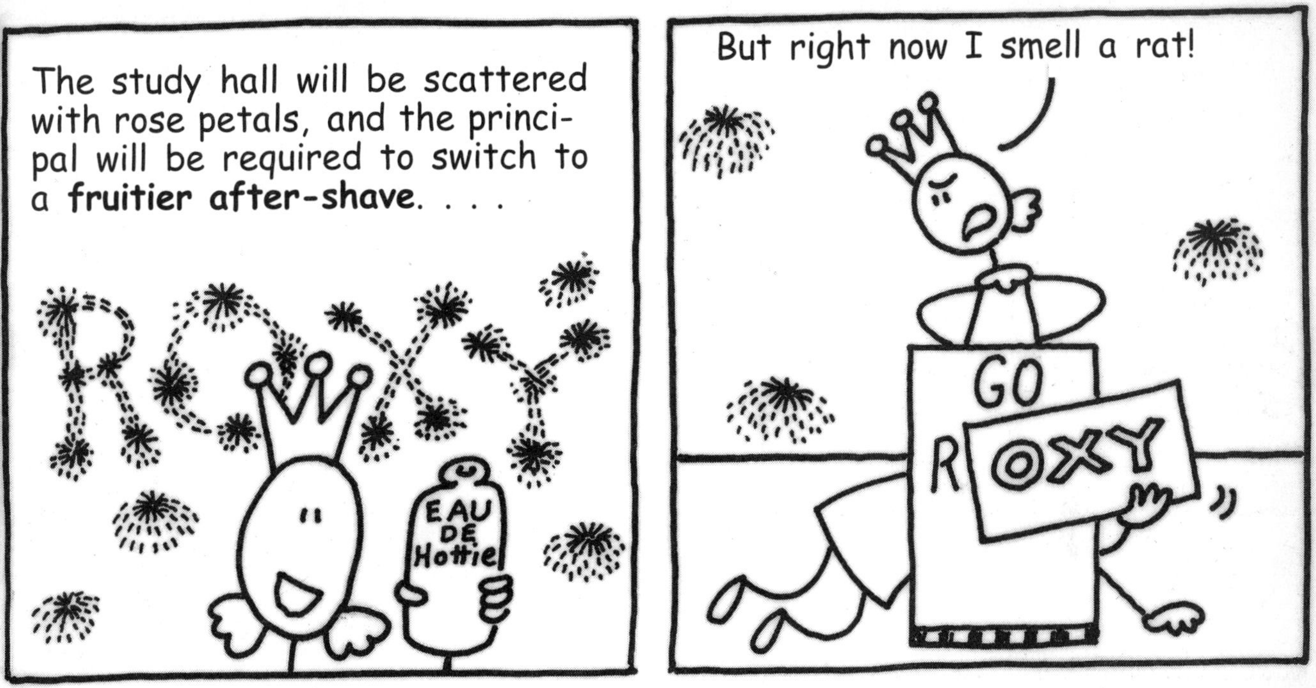
The study hall will be scattered with rose petals, and the principal will be required to switch to a **fruitier after-shave**. . . .
ROXY
EAU DE Hottie
But right now I smell a rat!
GO ROXY

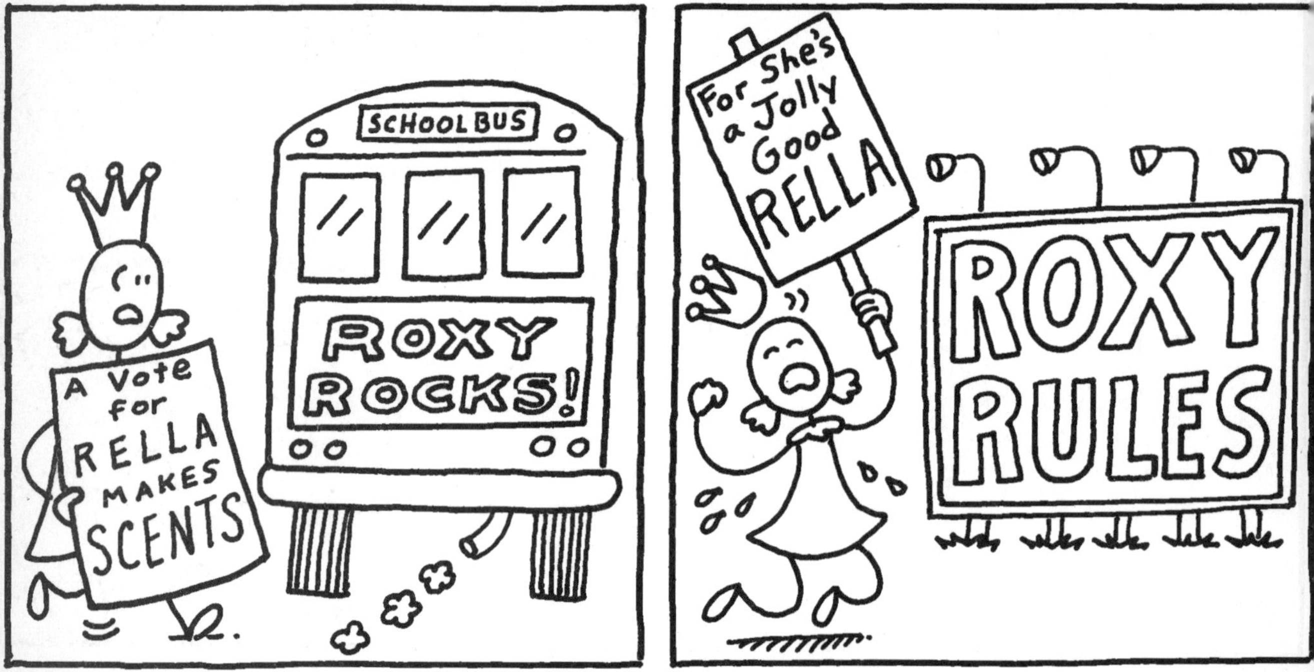
A Vote for RELLA MAKES SCENTS
SCHOOL BUS
ROXY ROCKS!
For She's a Jolly Good RELLA
ROXY RULES

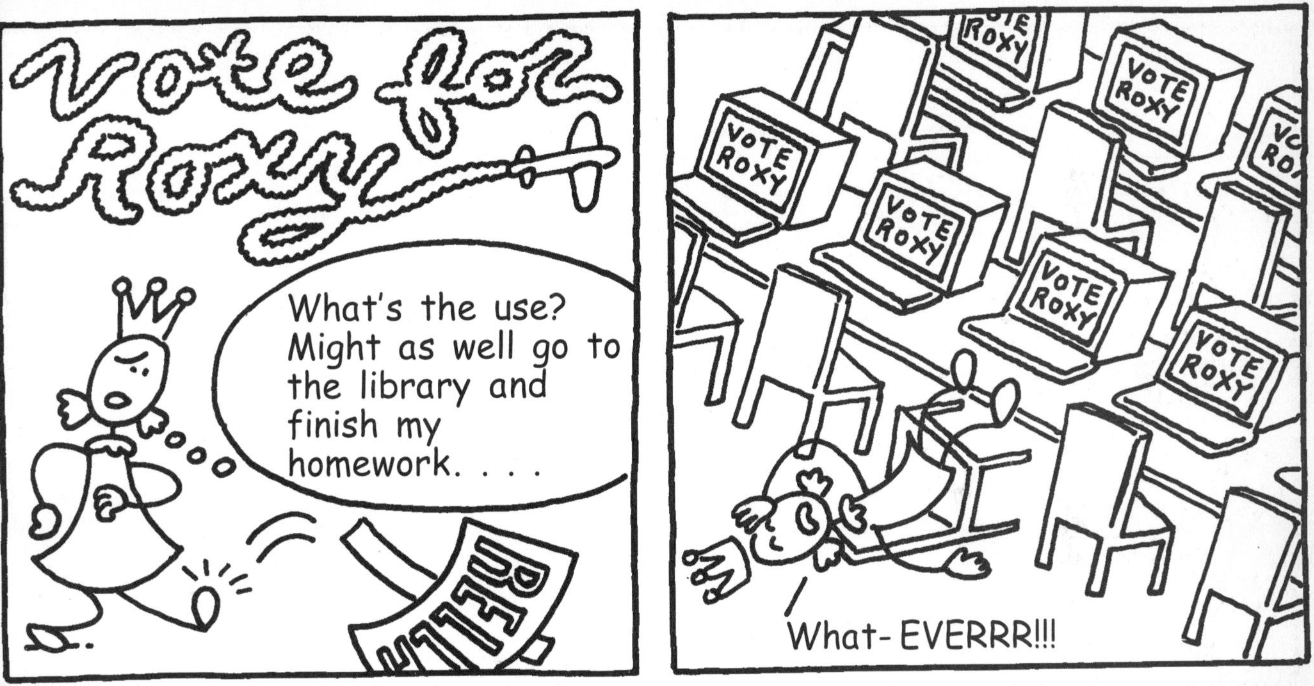

Vote for Roxy
What's the use? Might as well go to the library and finish my homework. . . .
VOTE ROXY
What-EVERRR!!!

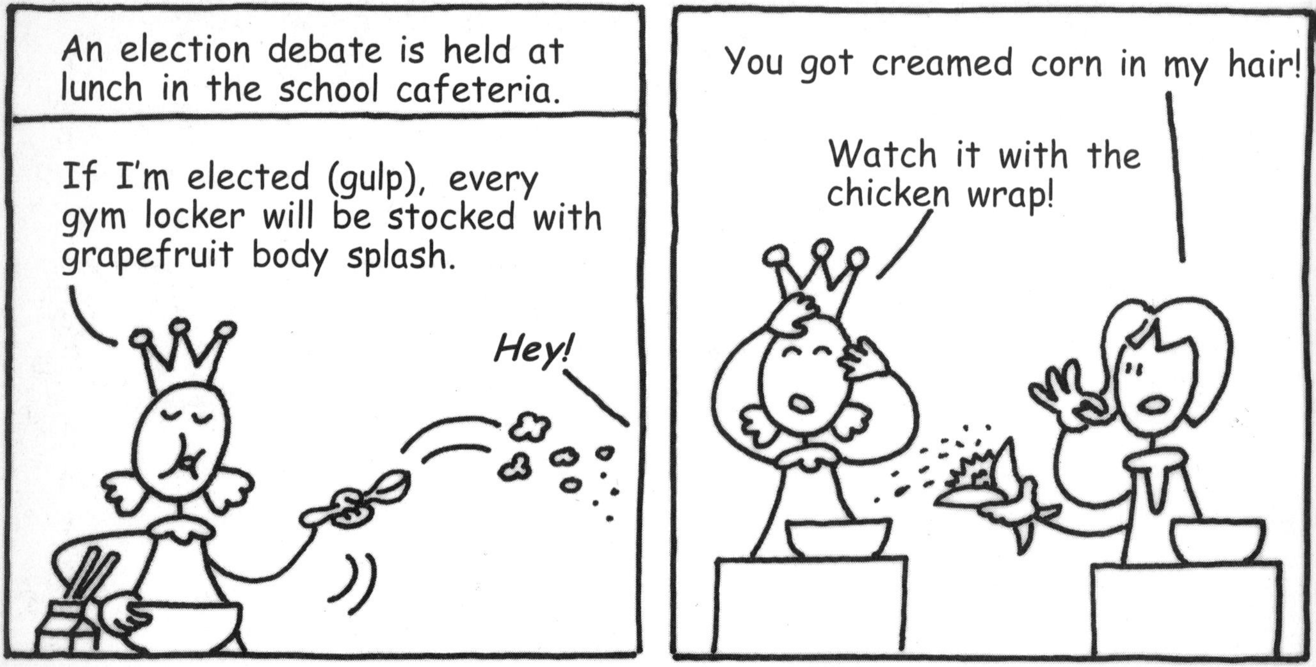
An election debate is held at lunch in the school cafeteria.
If I'm elected (gulp), every gym locker will be stocked with grapefruit body splash.
Hey!
You got creamed corn in my hair!
Watch it with the chicken wrap!

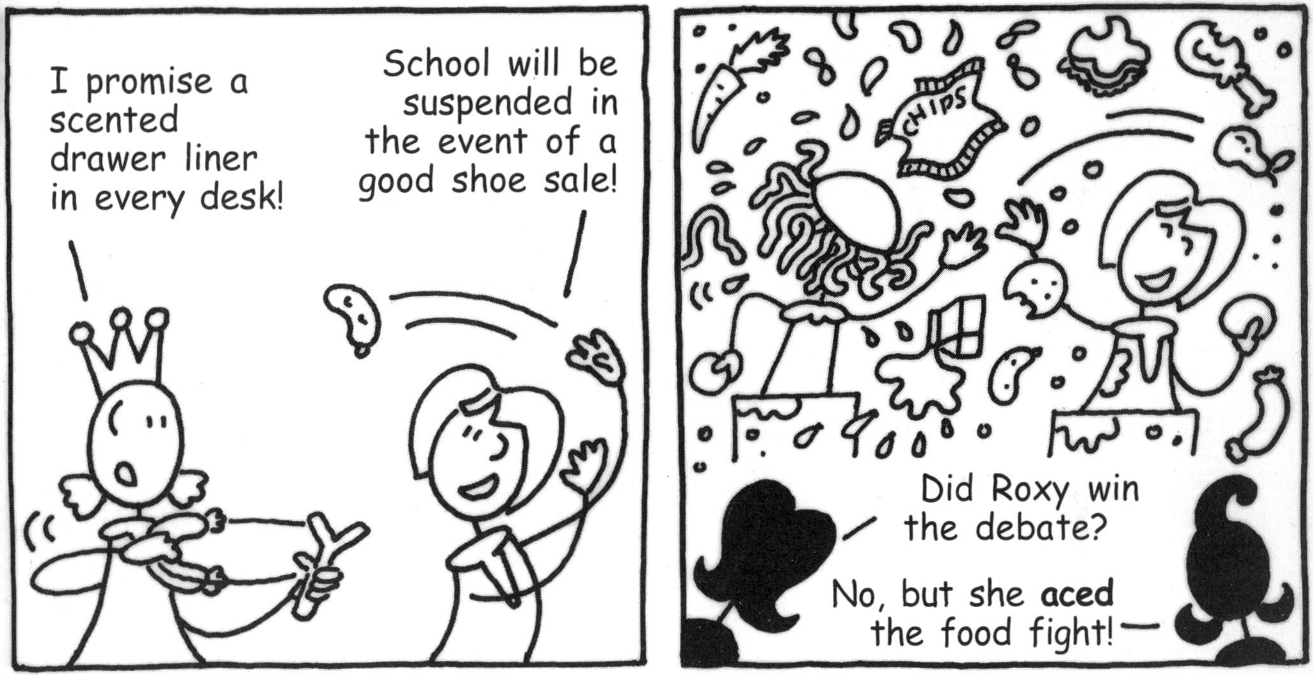
I promise a scented drawer liner in every desk!
School will be suspended in the event of a good shoe sale!
CHIPS
Did Roxy win the debate?
No, but she **aced** the food fight!

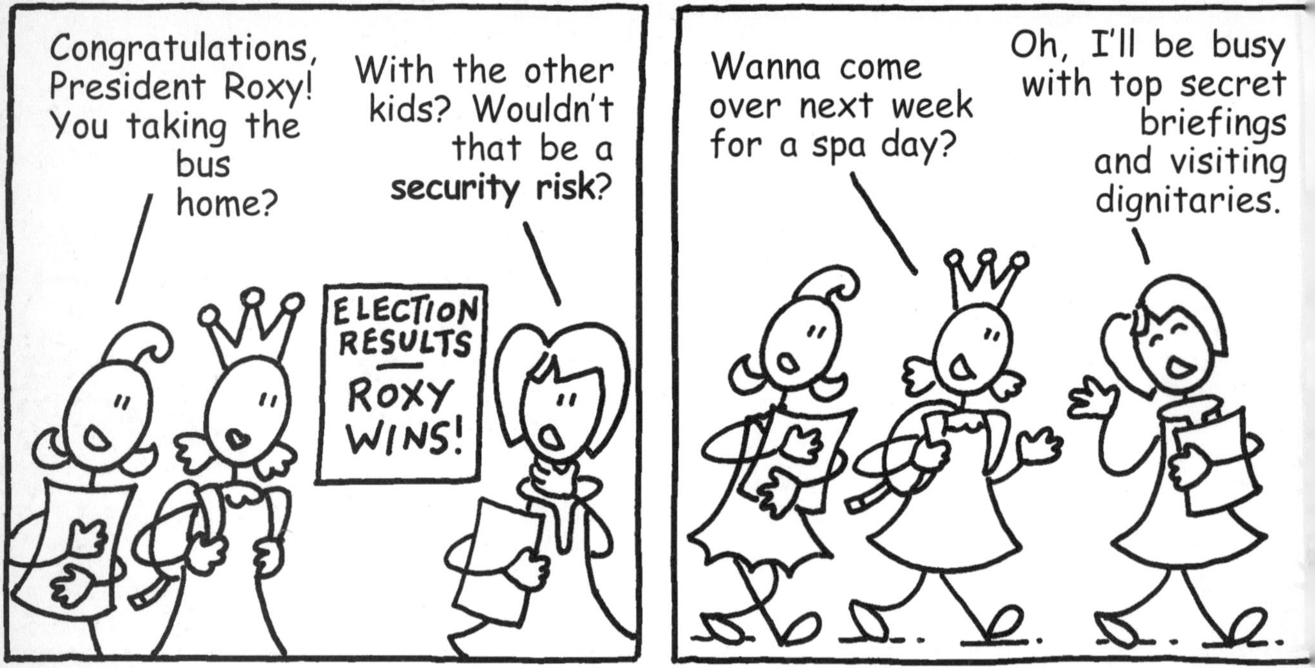
Congratulations, President Roxy! You taking the bus home?
With the other kids? Wouldn't that be a **security risk**?
ELECTION RESULTS — ROXY WINS!
Wanna come over next week for a spa day?
Oh, I'll be busy with top secret briefings and visiting dignitaries.

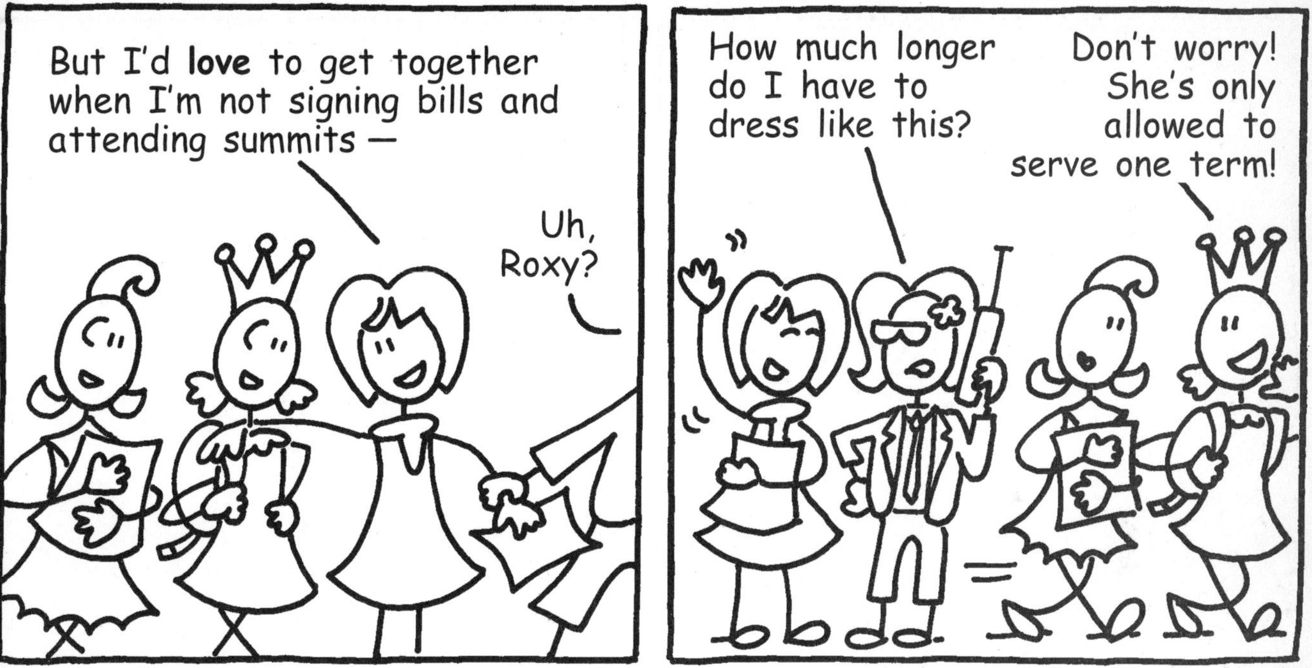
But I'd **love** to get together when I'm not signing bills and attending summits —
Uh, Roxy?
How much longer do I have to dress like this?
Don't worry! She's only allowed to serve one term!

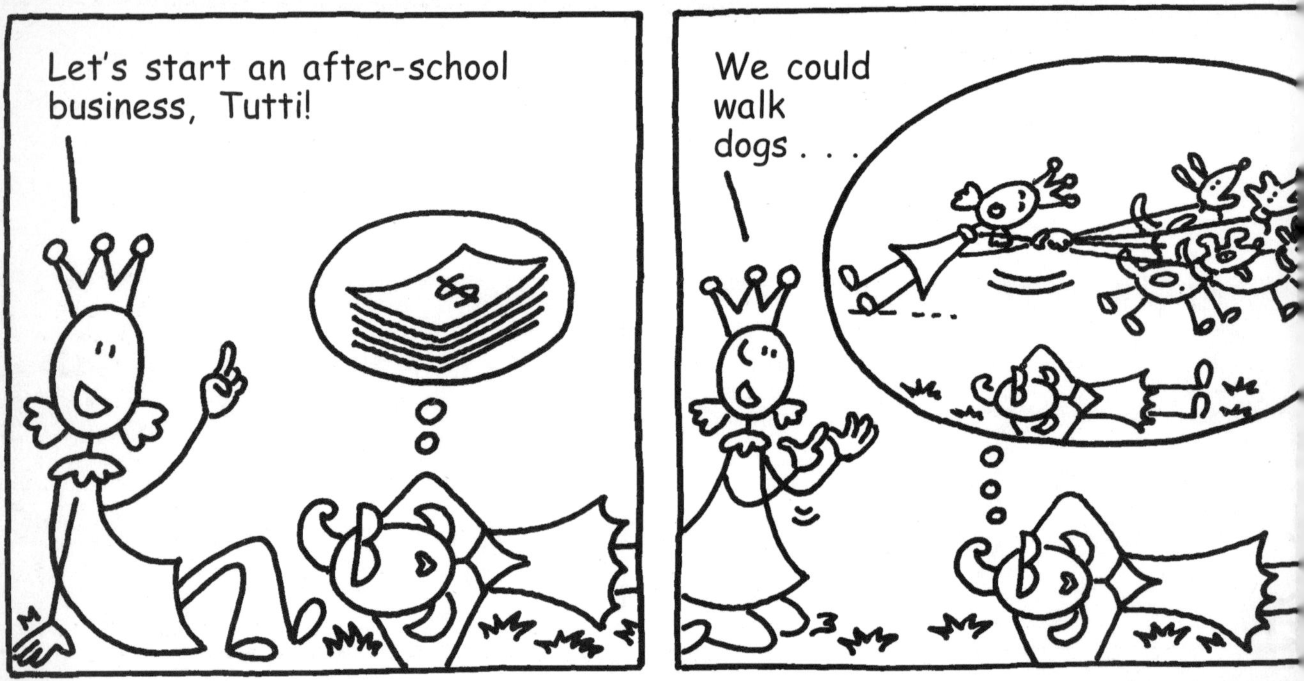
Let's start an after-school business, Tutti!
We could walk dogs . . .

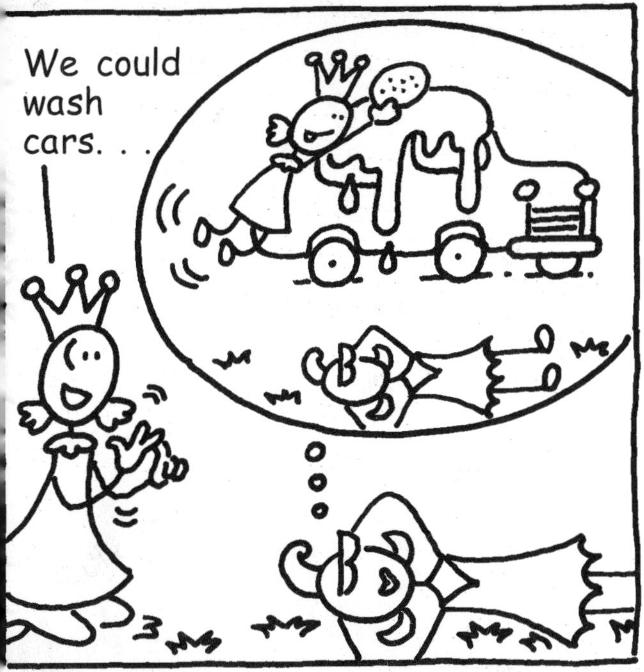
We could wash cars. . .

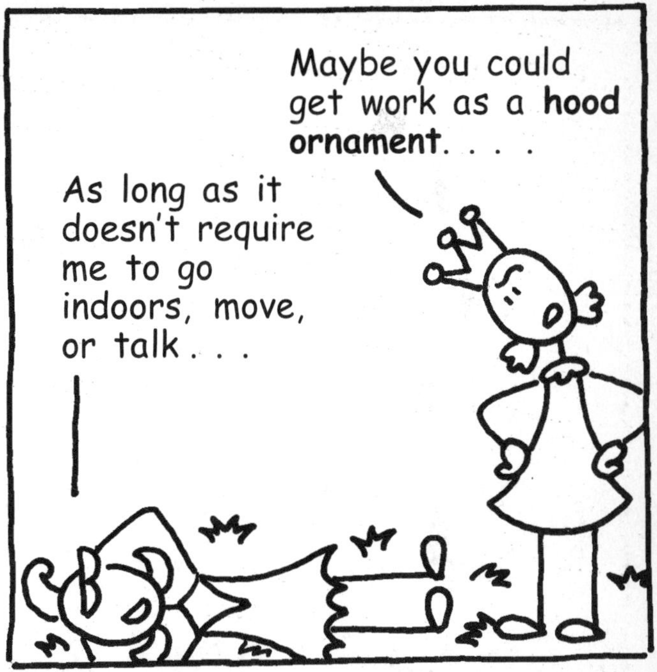
Maybe you could get work as a **hood ornament**. . . .
As long as it doesn't require me to go indoors, move, or talk . . .

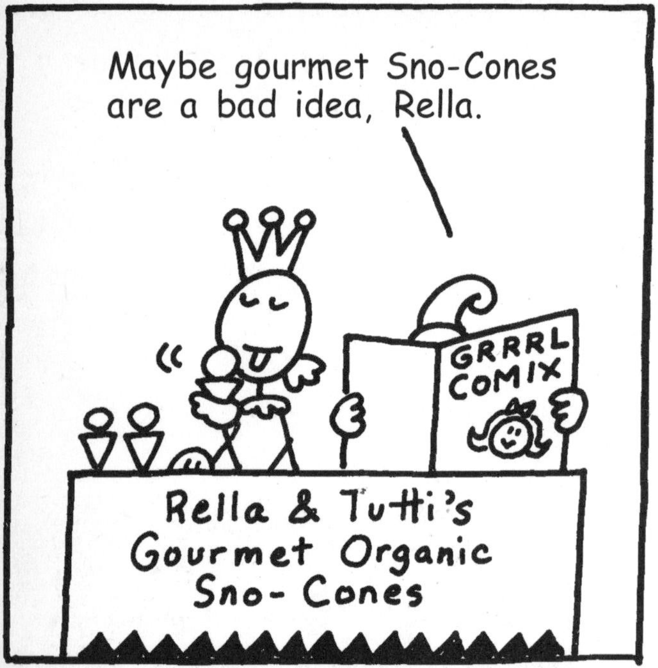
Maybe gourmet Sno-Cones are a bad idea, Rella.
GRRRL COMIX
Rella & Tutti's Gourmet Organic Sno-Cones

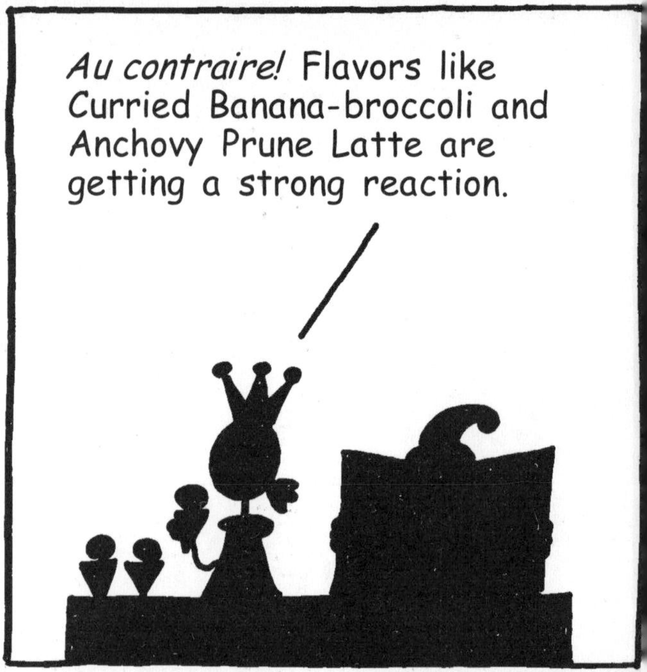
Au contraire! Flavors like Curried Banana-broccoli and Anchovy Prune Latte are getting a strong reaction.

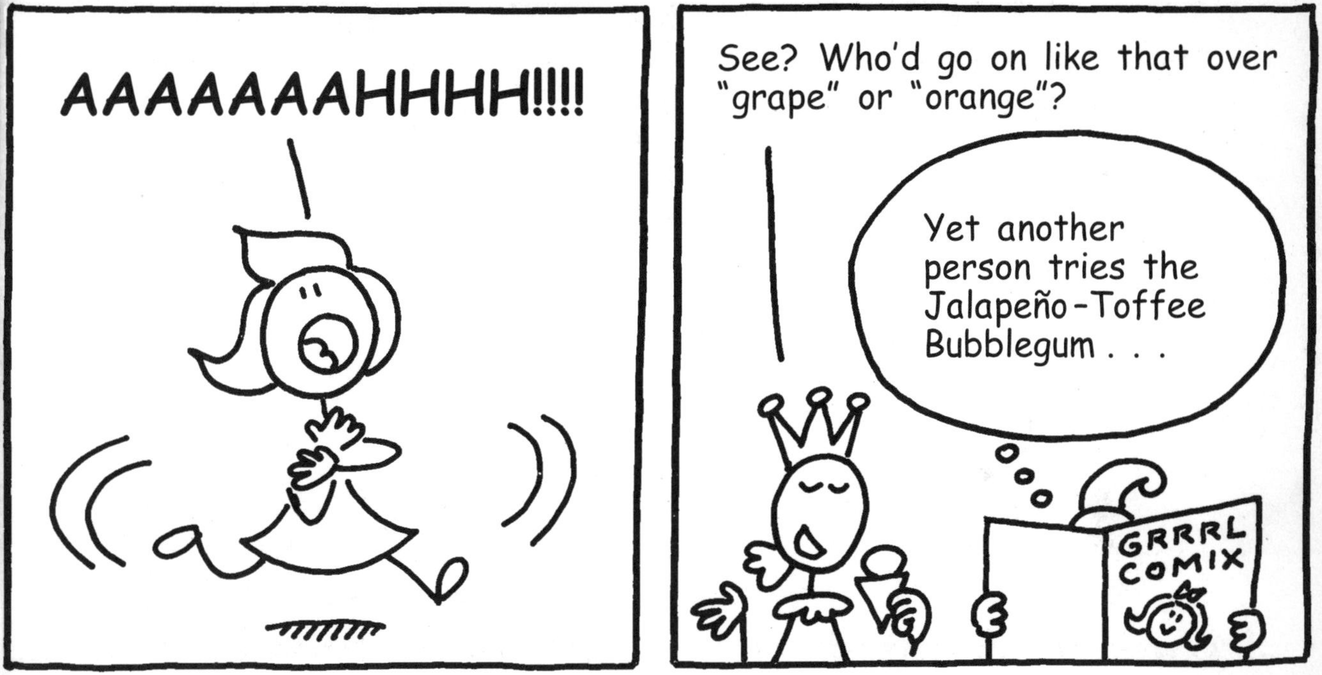
AAAAAAAHHHHH!!!!
See? Who'd go on like that over "grape" or "orange"?
Yet another person tries the Jalapeño-Toffee Bubblegum . . .
GRRRL COMIX

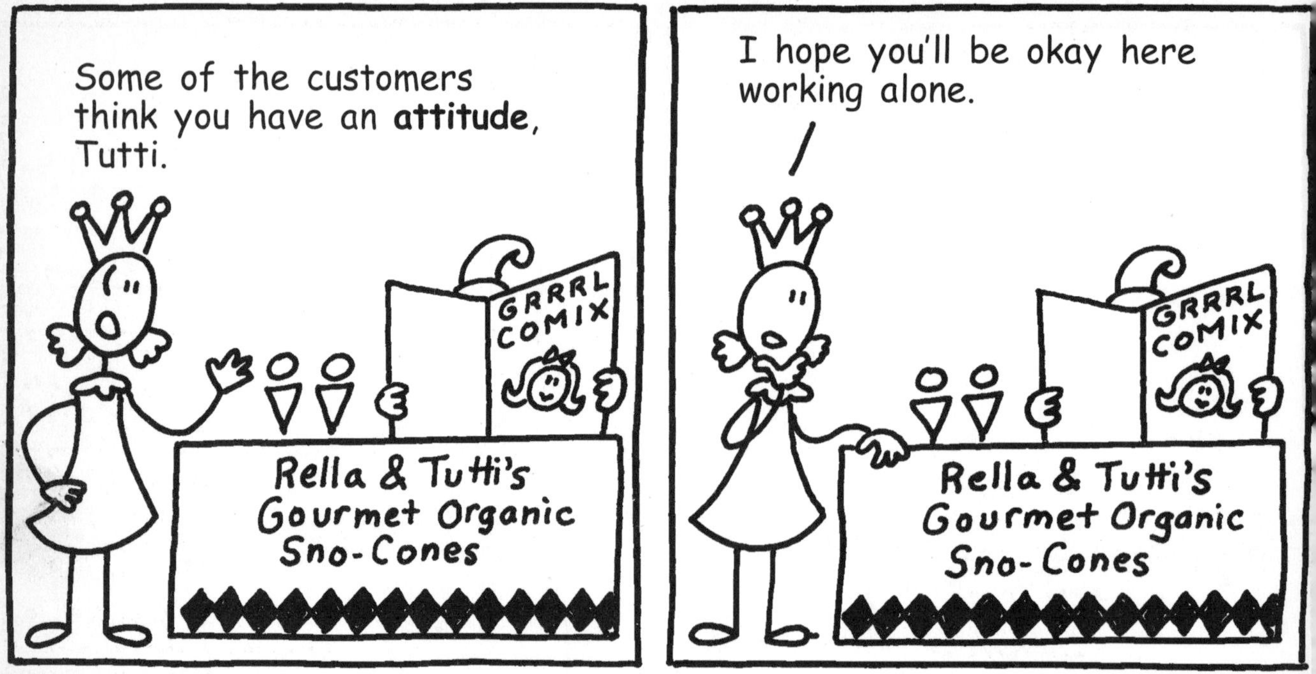
Some of the customers think you have an **attitude**, Tutti.
GRRRL COMIX
Rella & Tutti's Gourmet Organic Sno-Cones
I hope you'll be okay here working alone.
GRRRL COMIX
Rella & Tutti's Gourmet Organic Sno-Cones

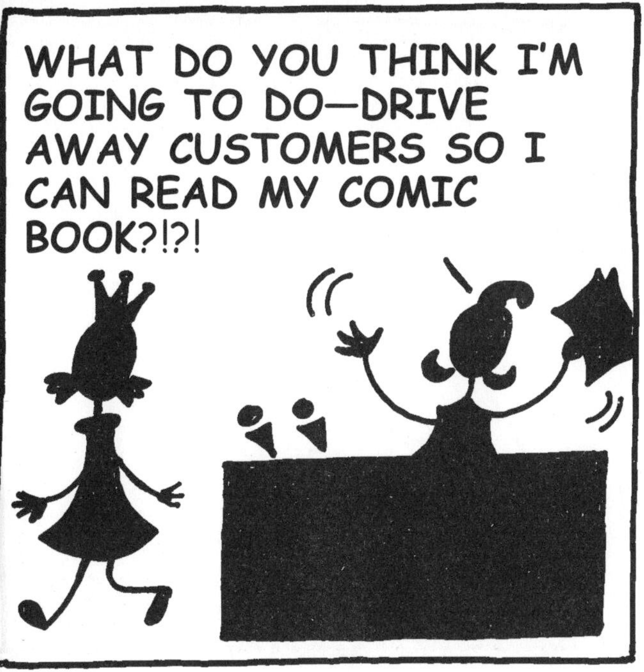
WHAT DO YOU THINK I'M GOING TO DO—DRIVE AWAY CUSTOMERS SO I CAN READ MY COMIC BOOK?!?!

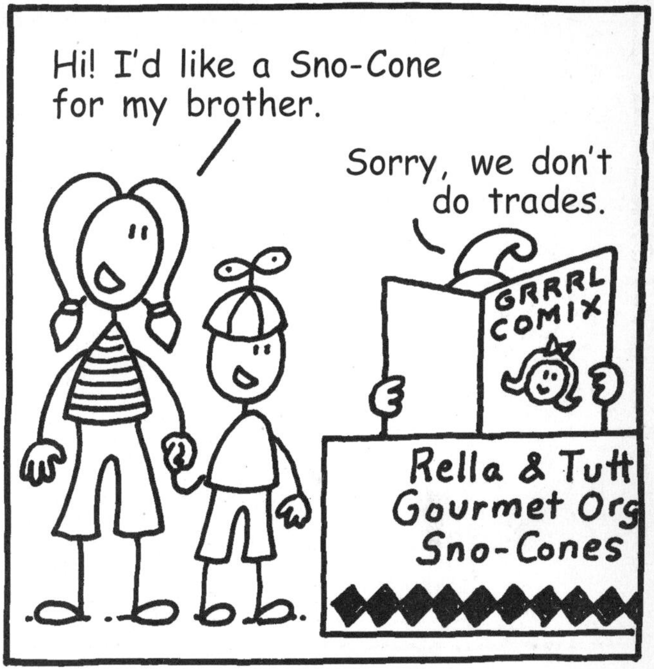
Hi! I'd like a Sno-Cone for my brother.
Sorry, we don't do trades.
GRRRL COMIX
Rella & Tutt Gourmet Org Sno-Cones

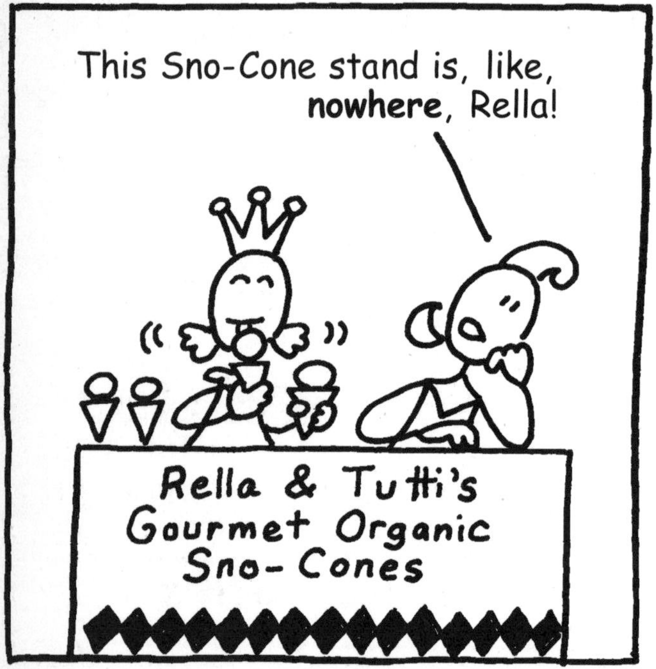
This Sno-Cone stand is, like, **nowhere**, Rella!
Rella & Tutti's Gourmet Organic Sno-Cones

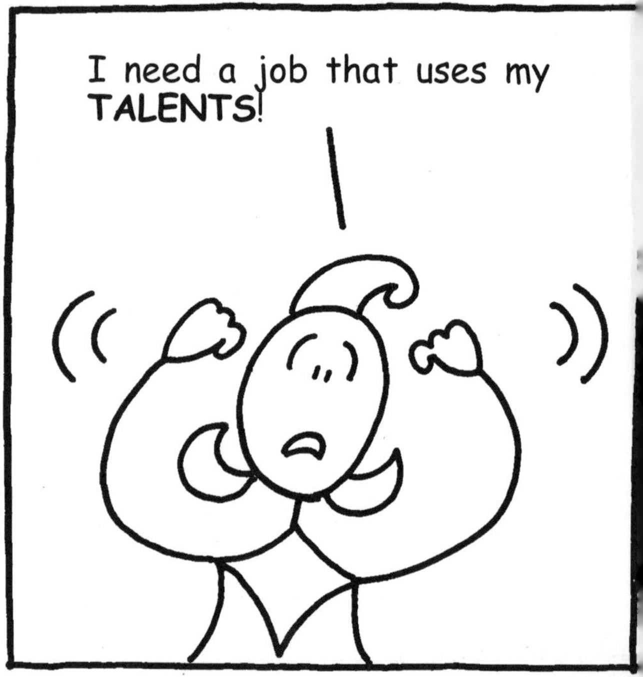
I need a job that uses my **TALENTS**!

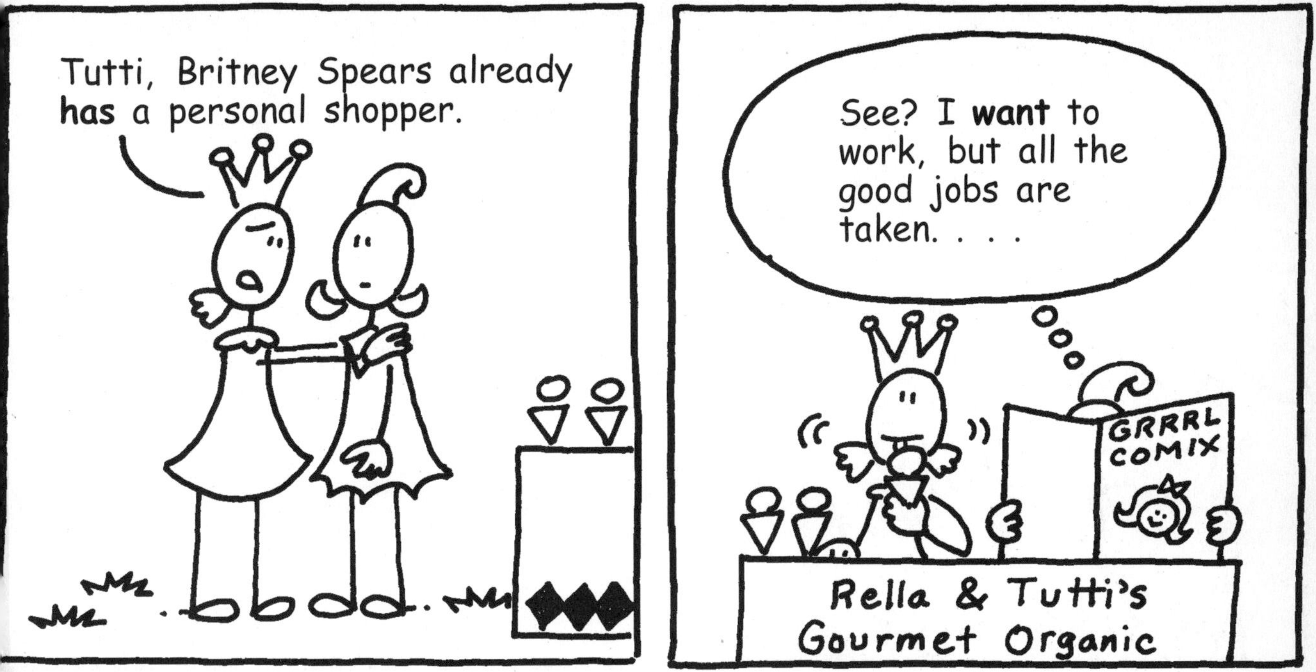
Tutti, Britney Spears already **has** a personal shopper.
See? I **want** to work, but all the good jobs are taken. . . .
GRRRL COMIX
Rella & Tutti's Gourmet Organic

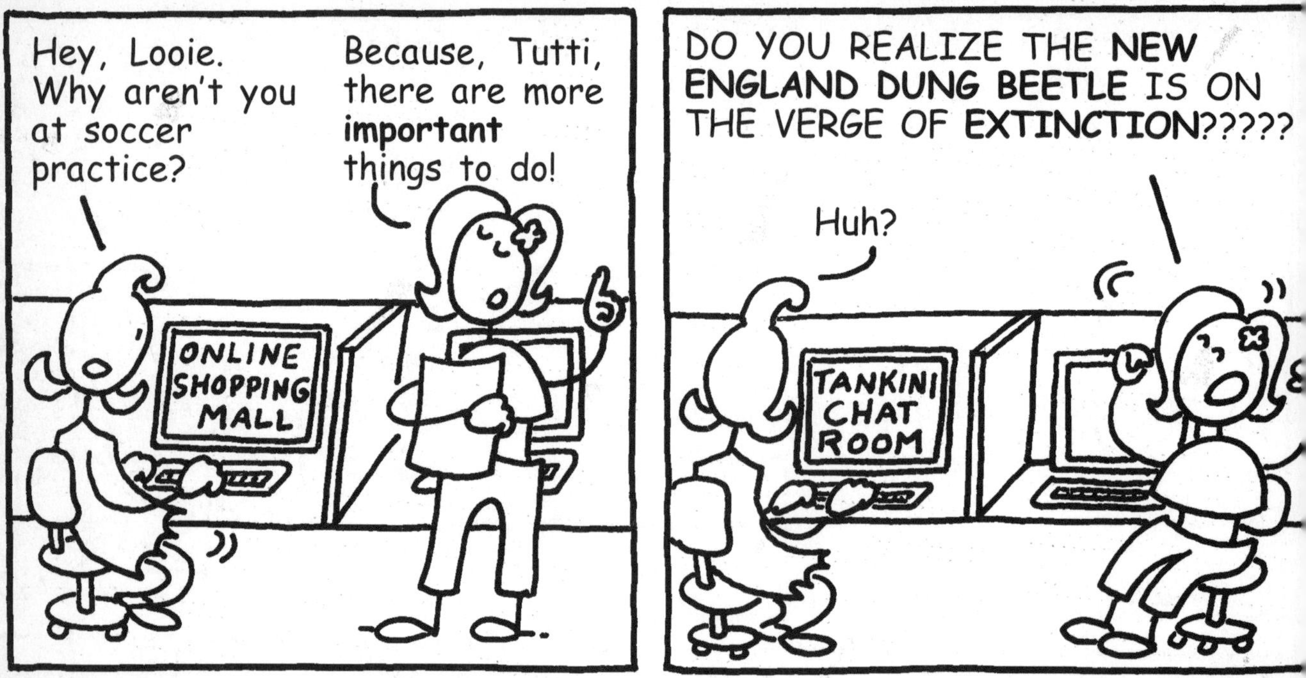
Hey, Looie. Why aren't you at soccer practice?
Because, Tutti, there are more **important** things to do!
ONLINE SHOPPING MALL
DO YOU REALIZE THE **NEW ENGLAND DUNG BEETLE** IS ON THE VERGE OF **EXTINCTION**?????
Huh?
TANKINI CHAT ROOM

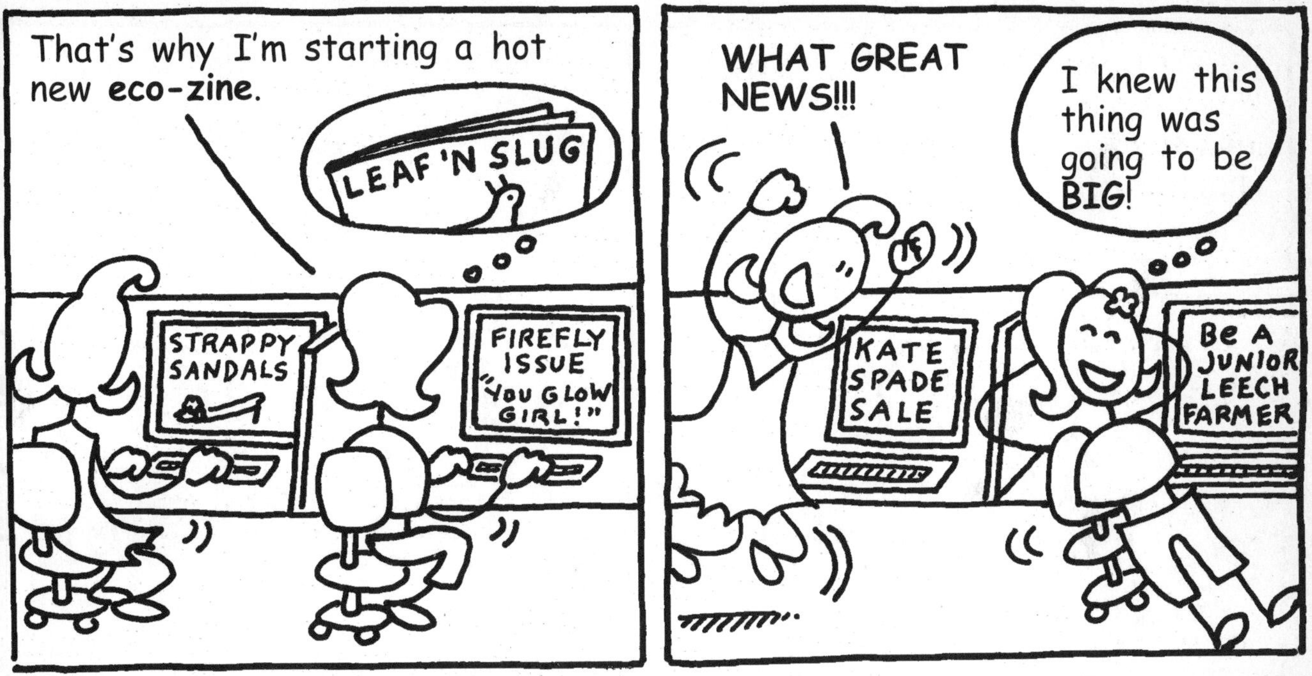
That's why I'm starting a hot new **eco-zine**.
LEAF 'N SLUG
STRAPPY SANDALS
FIREFLY ISSUE "YOU GLOW GIRL!"
WHAT GREAT NEWS!!!
I knew this thing was going to be **BIG**!
KATE SPADE SALE
Be A JUNIOR LEECH FARMER

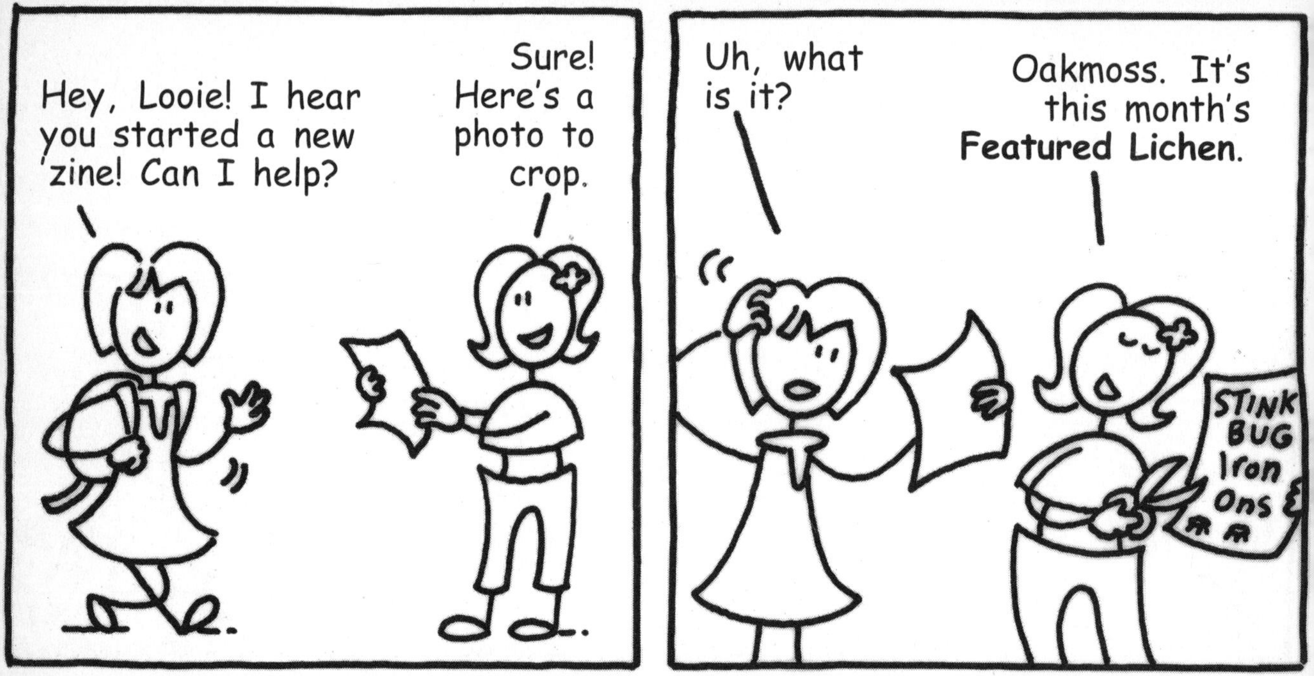
Hey, Looie! I hear you started a new 'zine! Can I help?
Sure! Here's a photo to crop.
Uh, what is it?
Oakmoss. It's this month's **Featured Lichen**.
STINK BUG Iron Ons

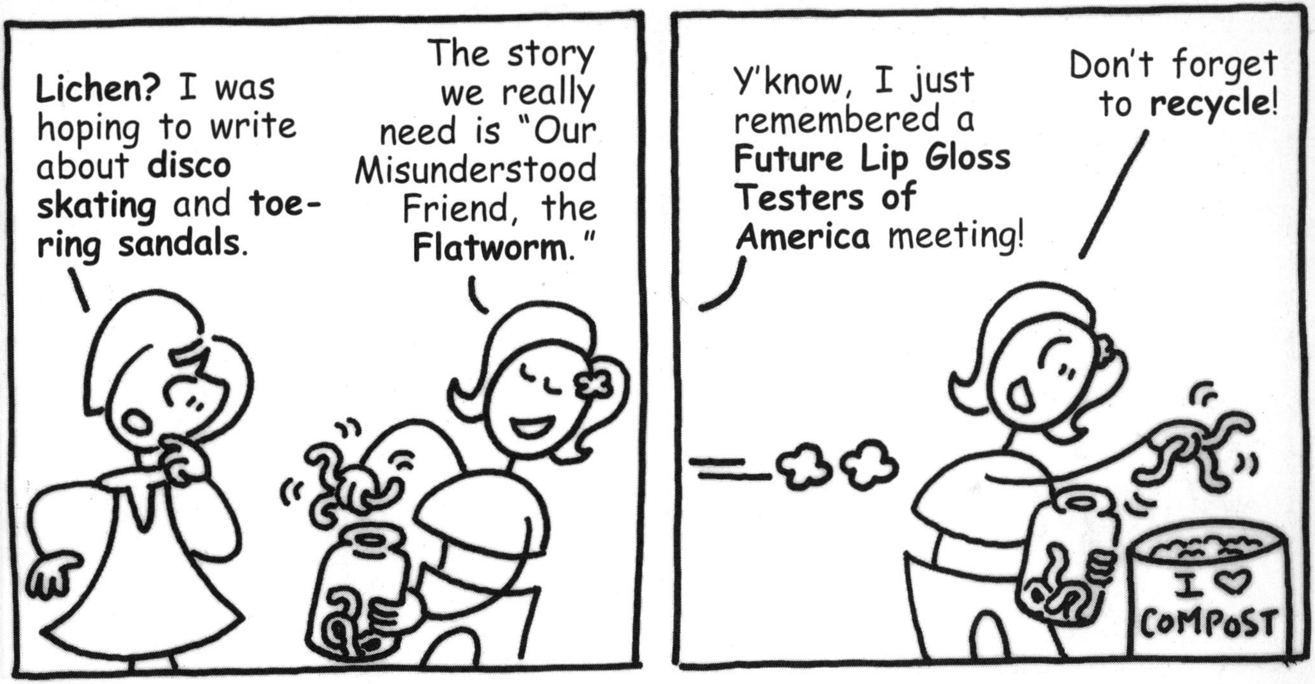
Lichen? I was hoping to write about disco skating and toe-ring sandals.
The story we really need is "Our Misunderstood Friend, the Flatworm."
Y'know, I just remembered a Future Lip Gloss Testers of America meeting!
Don't forget to recycle!
I ♡ COMPOST

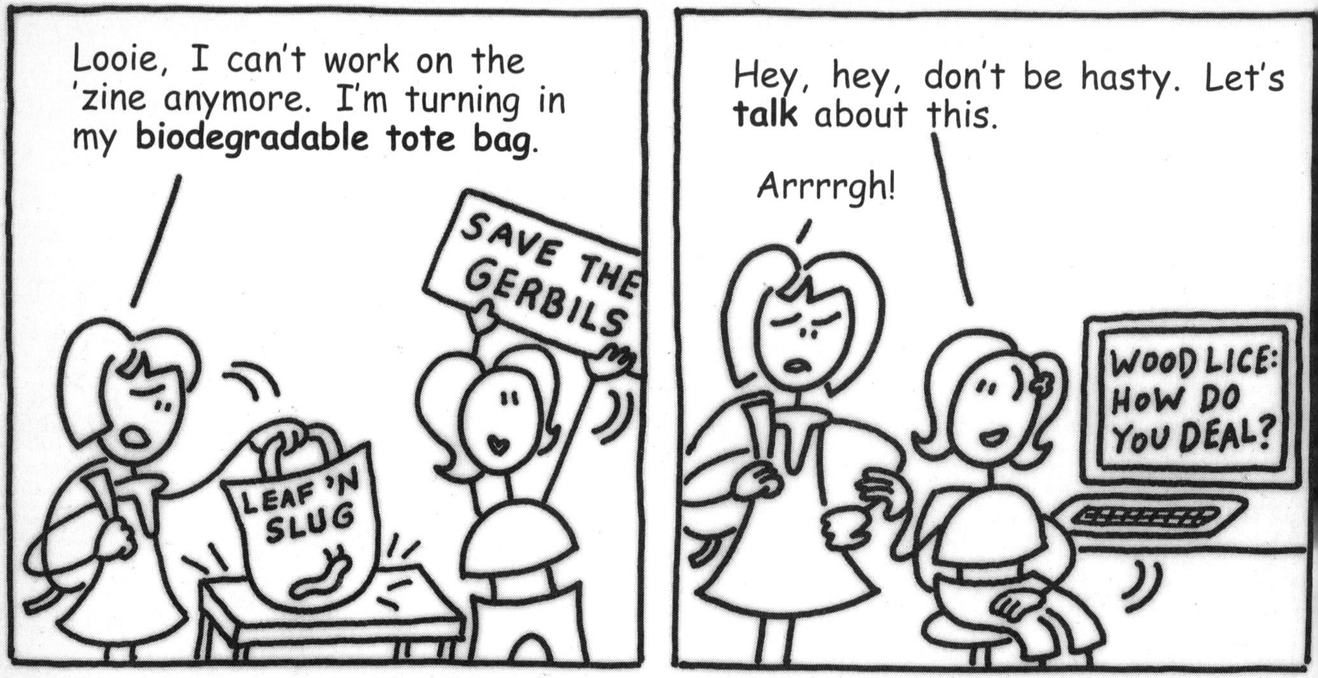
Looie, I can't work on the 'zine anymore. I'm turning in my **biodegradable tote bag**.
SAVE THE GERBILS
LEAF 'N SLUG
Hey, hey, don't be hasty. Let's **talk** about this.
Arrrrgh!
WOOD LICE: HOW DO YOU DEAL?

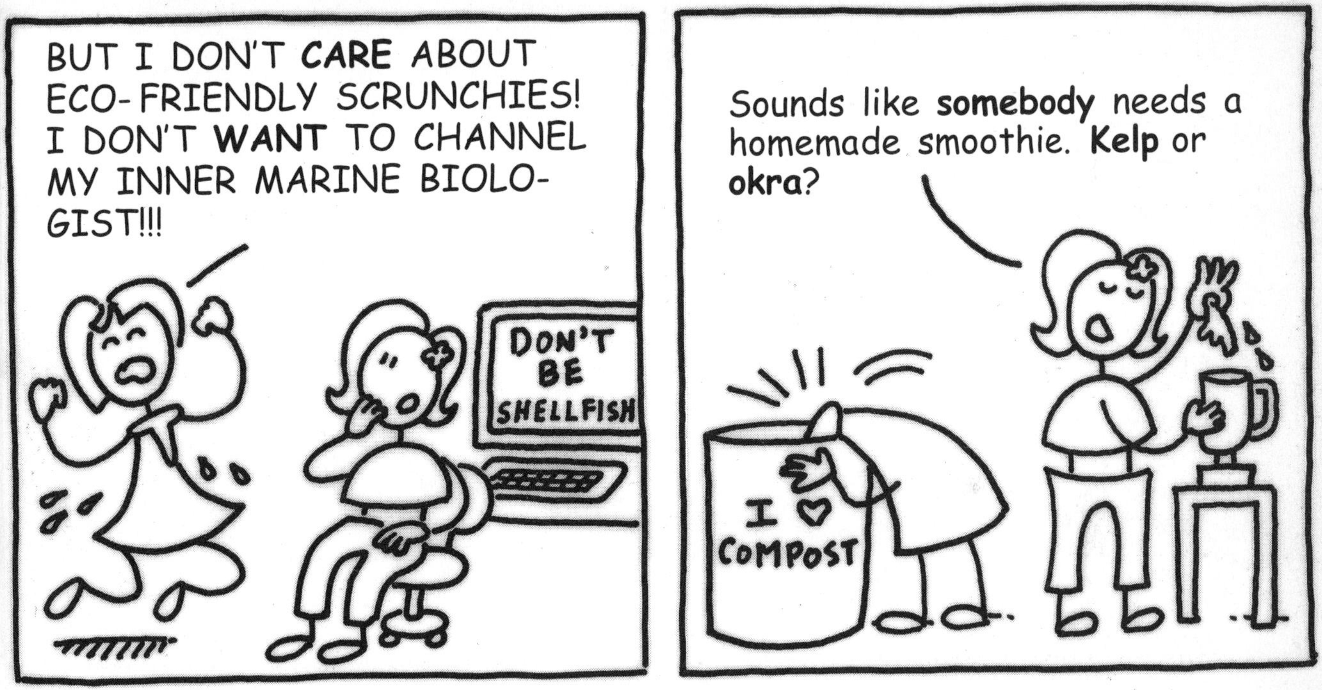
BUT I DON'T **CARE** ABOUT ECO-FRIENDLY SCRUNCHIES! I DON'T **WANT** TO CHANNEL MY INNER MARINE BIOLOGIST!!!
DON'T BE SHELLFISH
Sounds like **somebody** needs a homemade smoothie. **Kelp** or **okra**?
I ♥ COMPOST

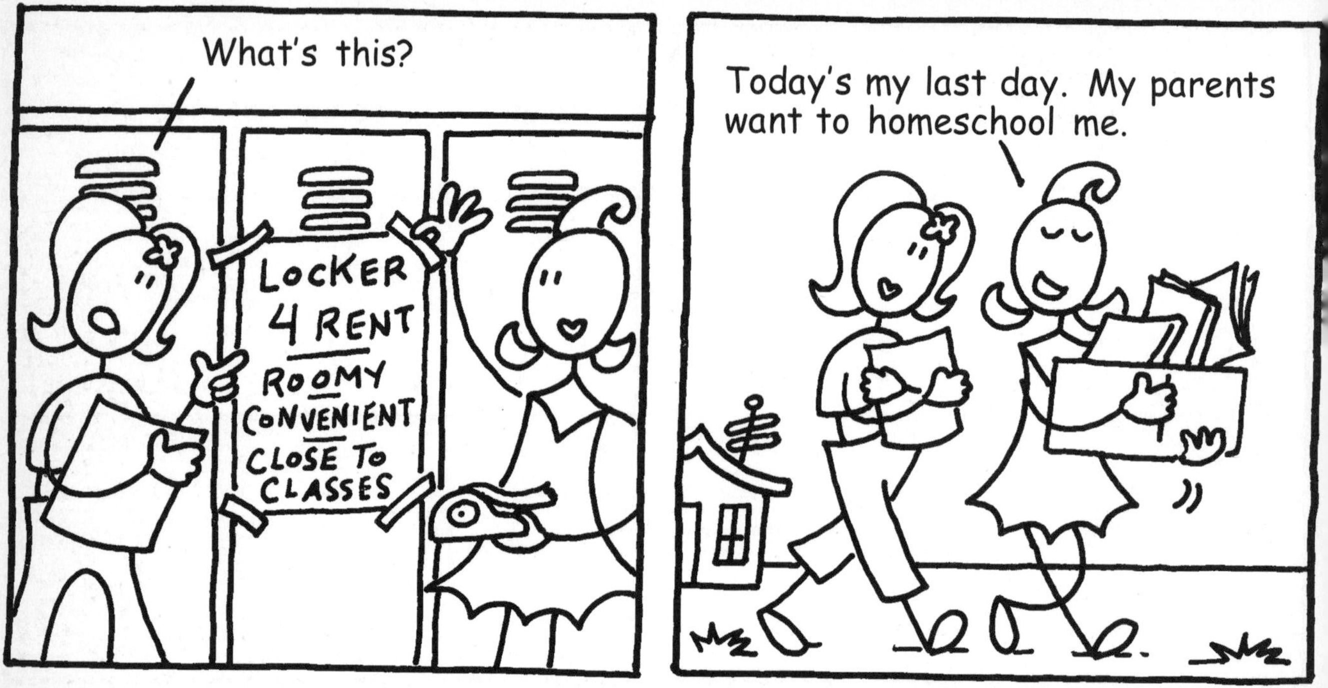
What's this?
LOCKER 4 RENT
ROOMY
CONVENIENT
CLOSE TO CLASSES
Today's my last day. My parents want to homeschool me.

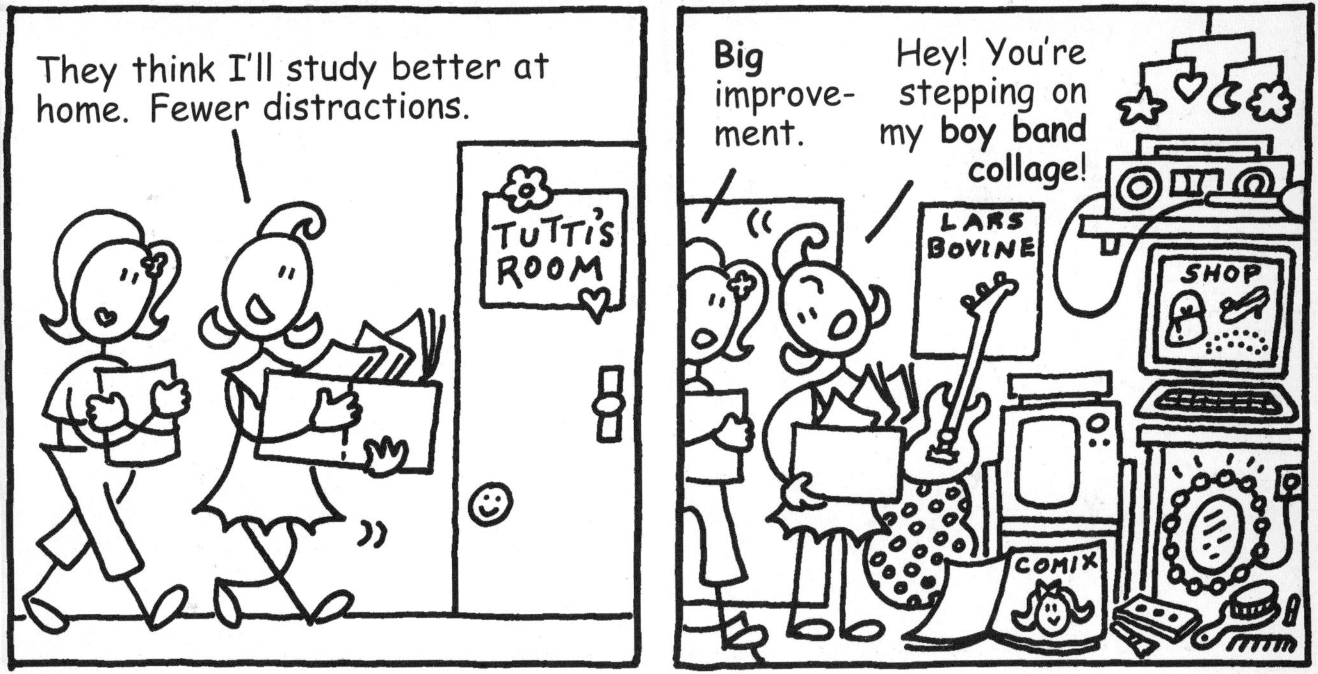
They think I'll study better at home. Fewer distractions.
TUTTI'S ROOM
Big improve-ment.
Hey! You're stepping on my boy band collage!
LARS BOVINE
SHOP
COMIX

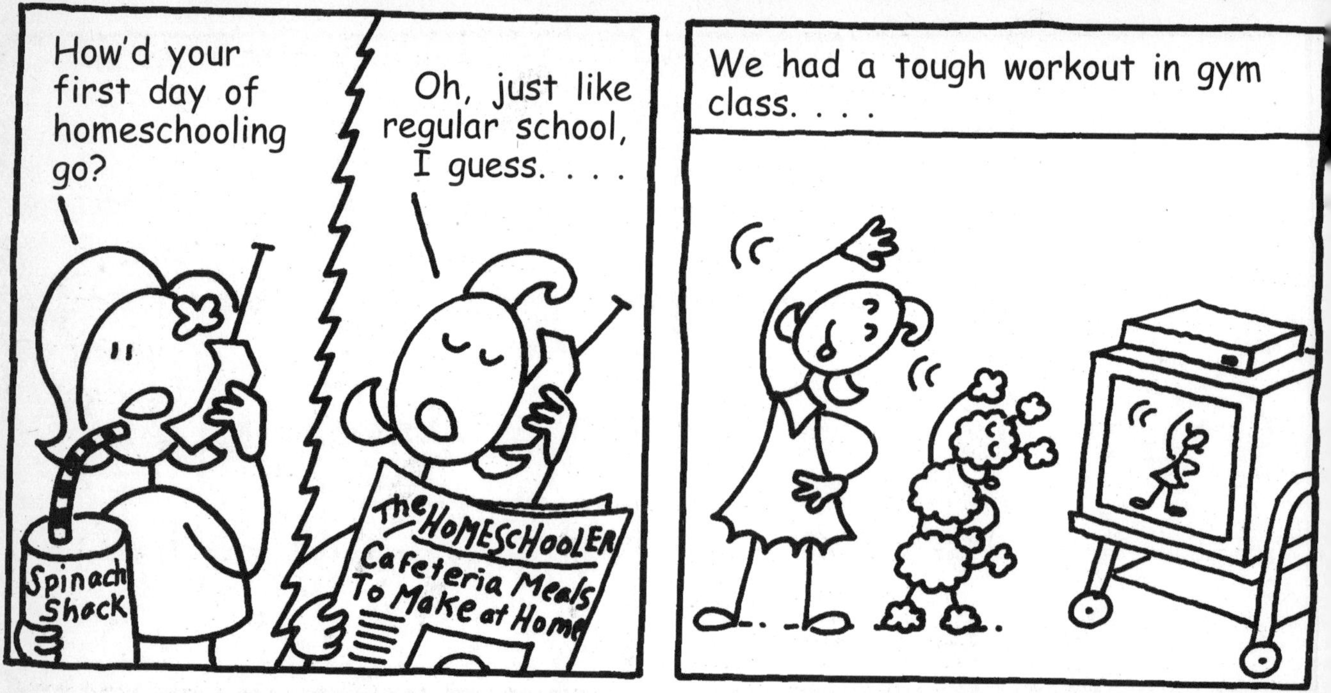
How'd your first day of homeschooling go?
Oh, just like regular school, I guess. . . .
Spinach Shack
The HOMESCHOOLER
Cafeteria Meals To Make at Home
We had a tough workout in gym class. . . .

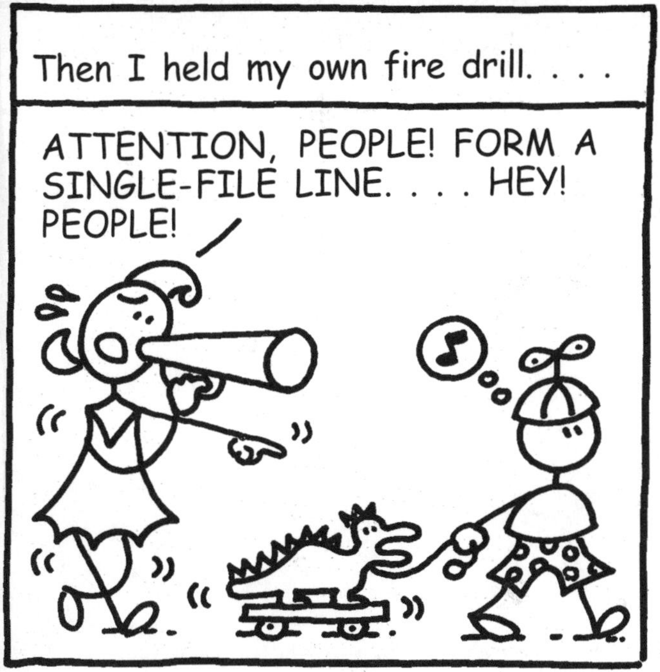
Then I held my own fire drill. . . .
ATTENTION, PEOPLE! FORM A SINGLE-FILE LINE. . . . HEY! PEOPLE!

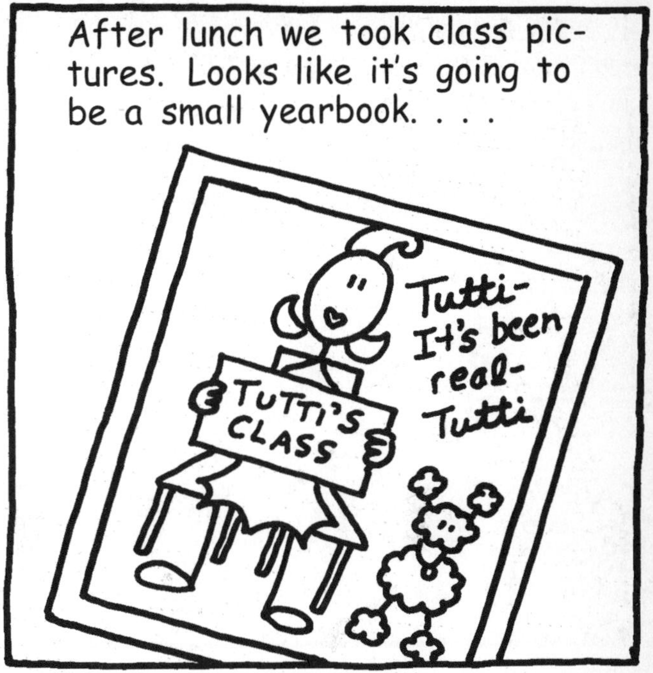
After lunch we took class pictures. Looks like it's going to be a small yearbook. . . .
TUTTI'S CLASS
Tutti-
It's been
real-
Tutti

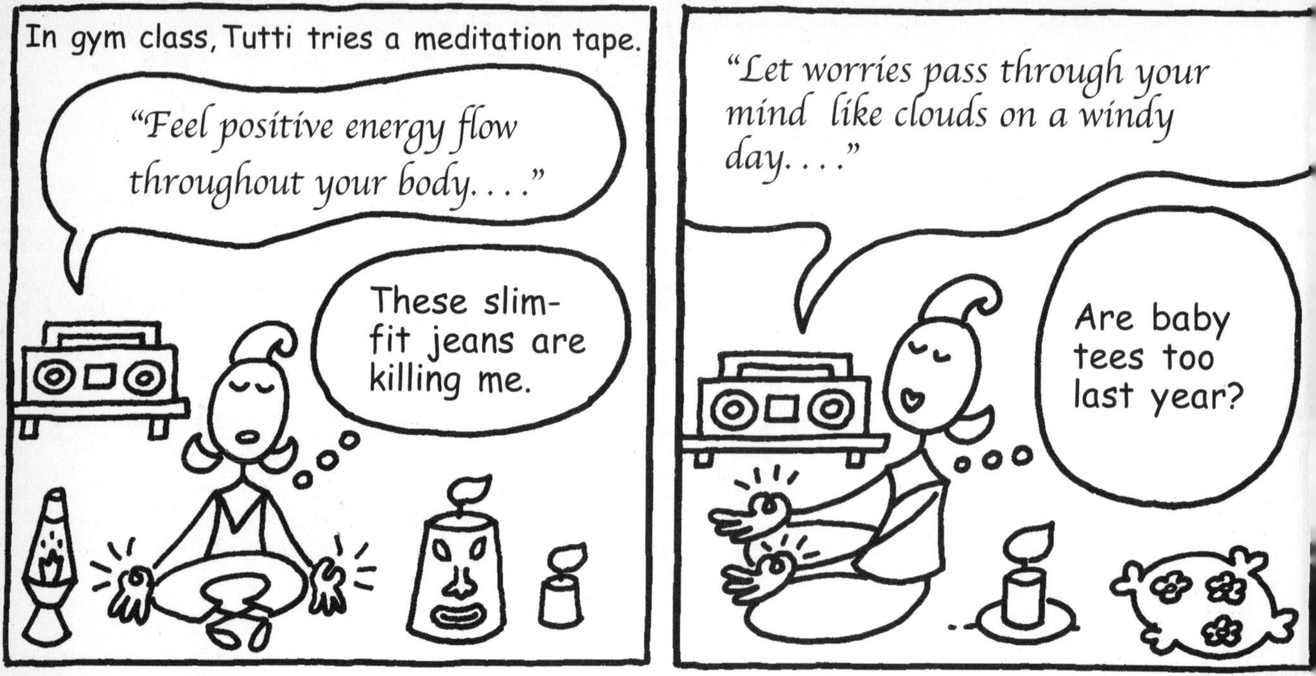
In gym class, Tutti tries a meditation tape.
"Feel positive energy flow throughout your body. . . ."
These slim-fit jeans are killing me.
"Let worries pass through your mind like clouds on a windy day. . . ."
Are baby tees too last year?

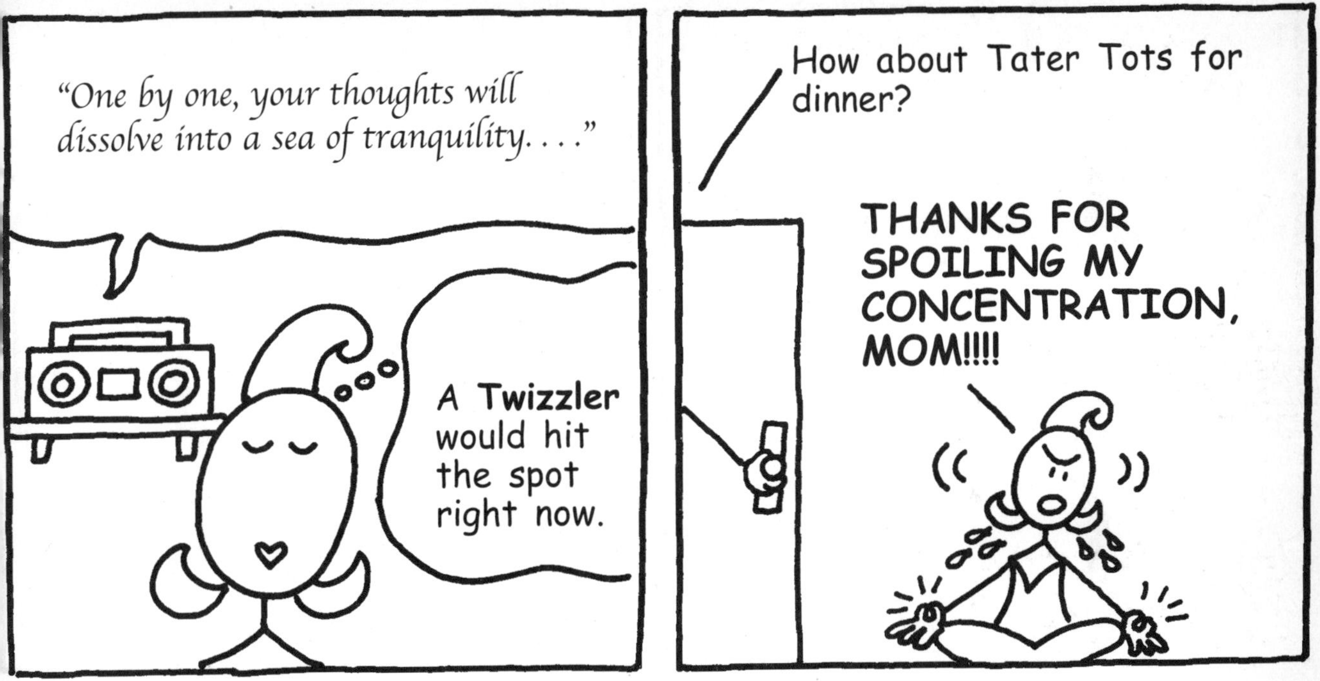
"One by one, your thoughts will dissolve into a sea of tranquility. . . ."
A **Twizzler** would hit the spot right now.
How about Tater Tots for dinner?
THANKS FOR SPOILING MY CONCENTRATION, MOM!!!!

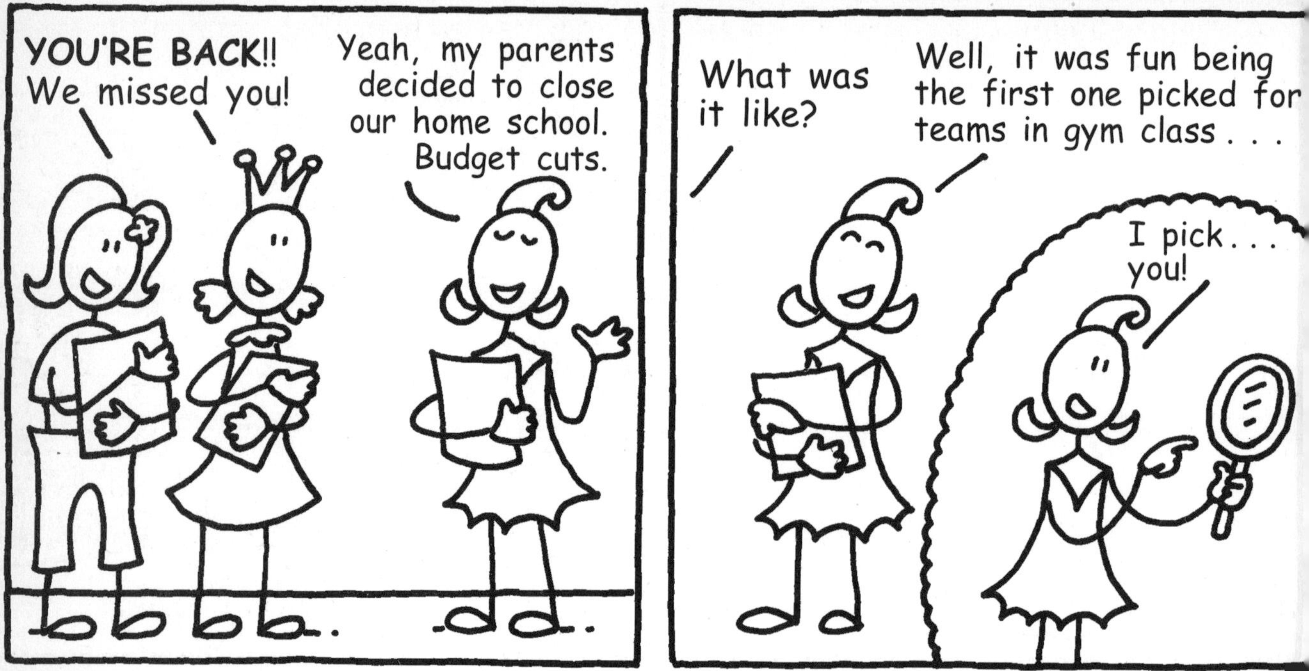
YOU'RE BACK!! We missed you!
Yeah, my parents decided to close our home school. Budget cuts.
What was it like?
Well, it was fun being the first one picked for teams in gym class . . .
I pick . . . you!

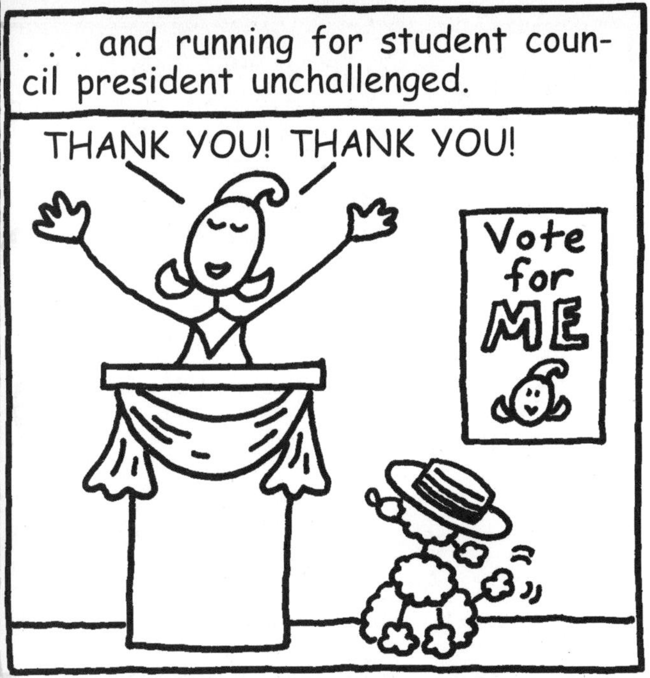
. . . and running for student council president unchallenged.
THANK YOU! THANK YOU!
Vote for ME

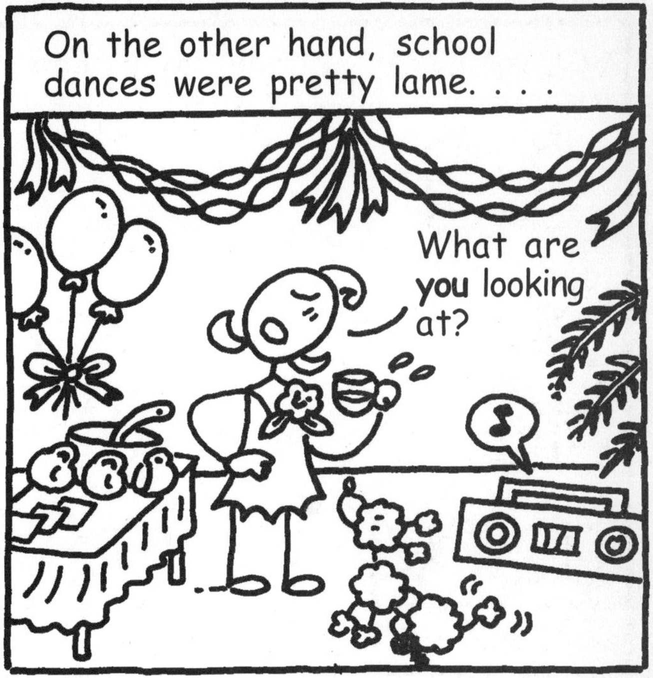
On the other hand, school dances were pretty lame. . . .
What are you looking at?

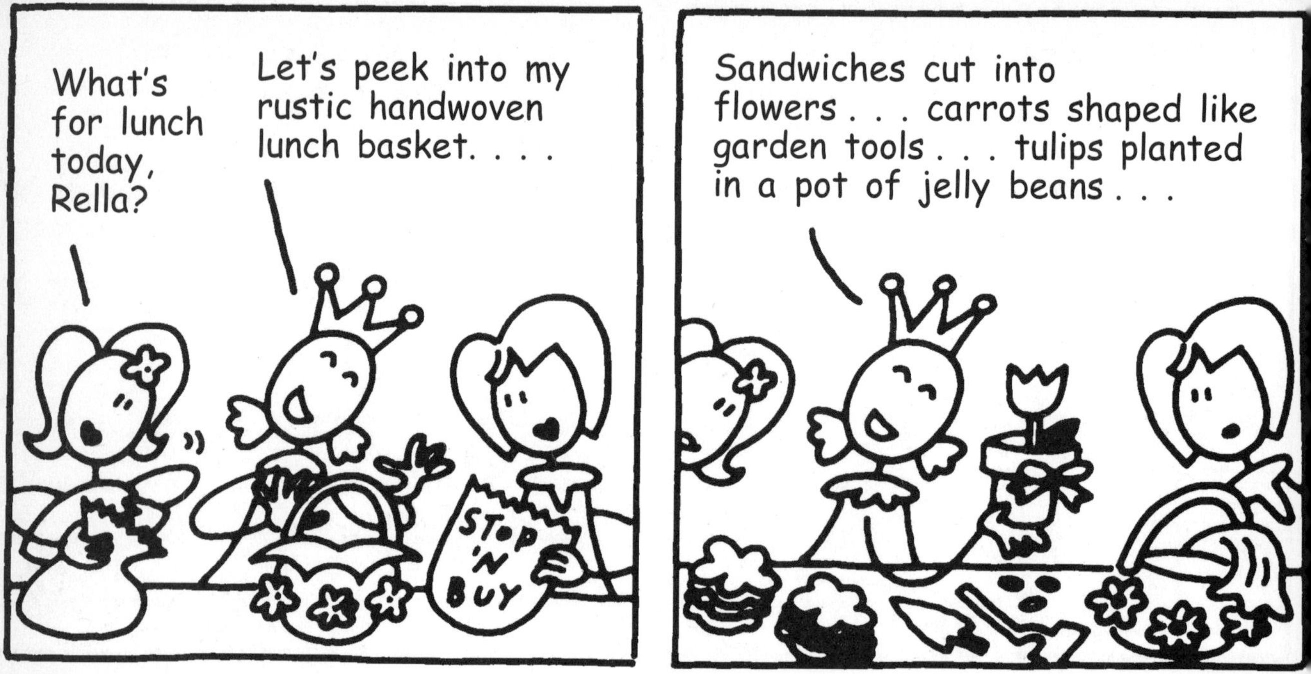
What's for lunch today, Rella?
Let's peek into my rustic handwoven lunch basket. . . .
STOP 'N BUY
Sandwiches cut into flowers . . . carrots shaped like garden tools . . . tulips planted in a pot of jelly beans . . .

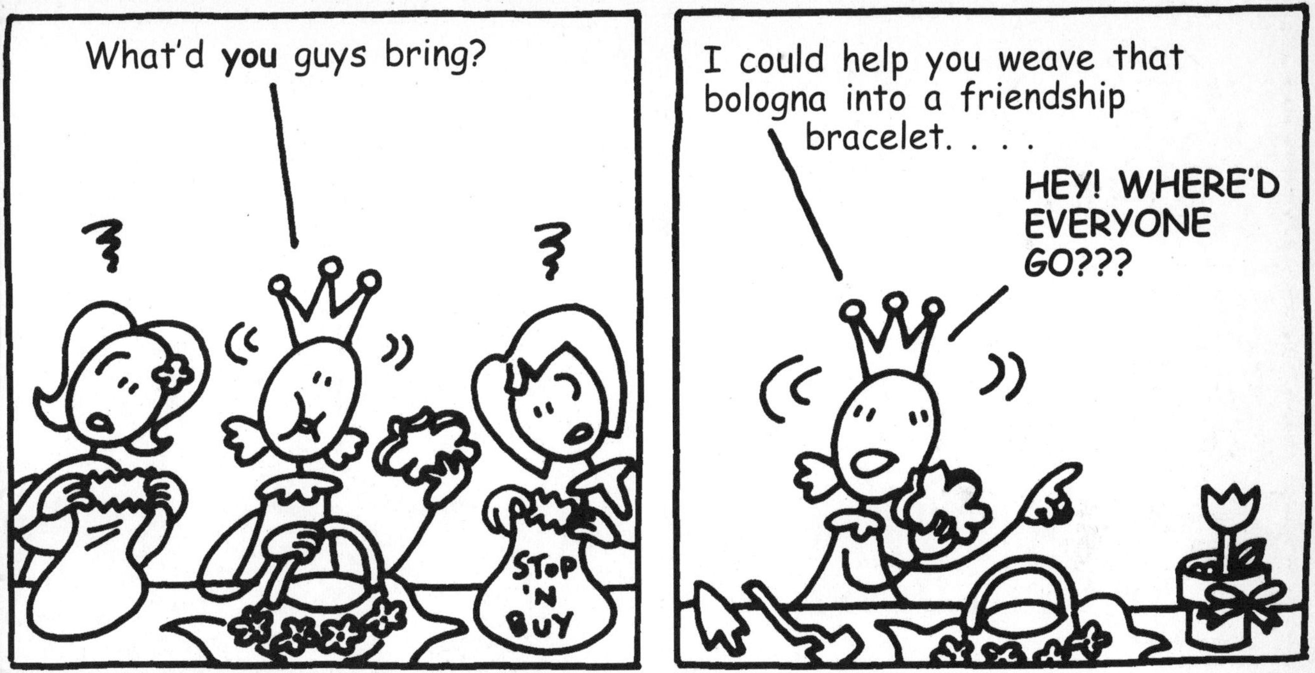
What'd **you** guys bring?
STOP 'N BUY
I could help you weave that bologna into a friendship bracelet. . . .
HEY! WHERE'D EVERYONE GO???

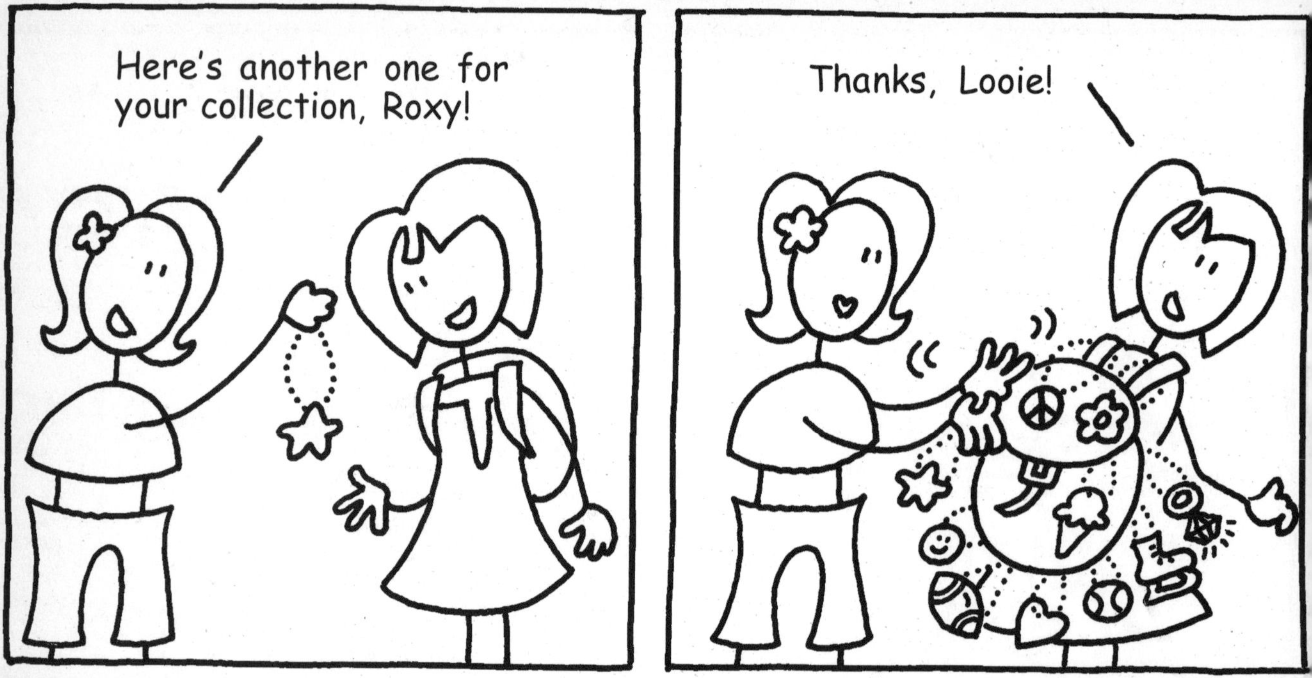
Here's another one for your collection, Roxy!
Thanks, Looie!

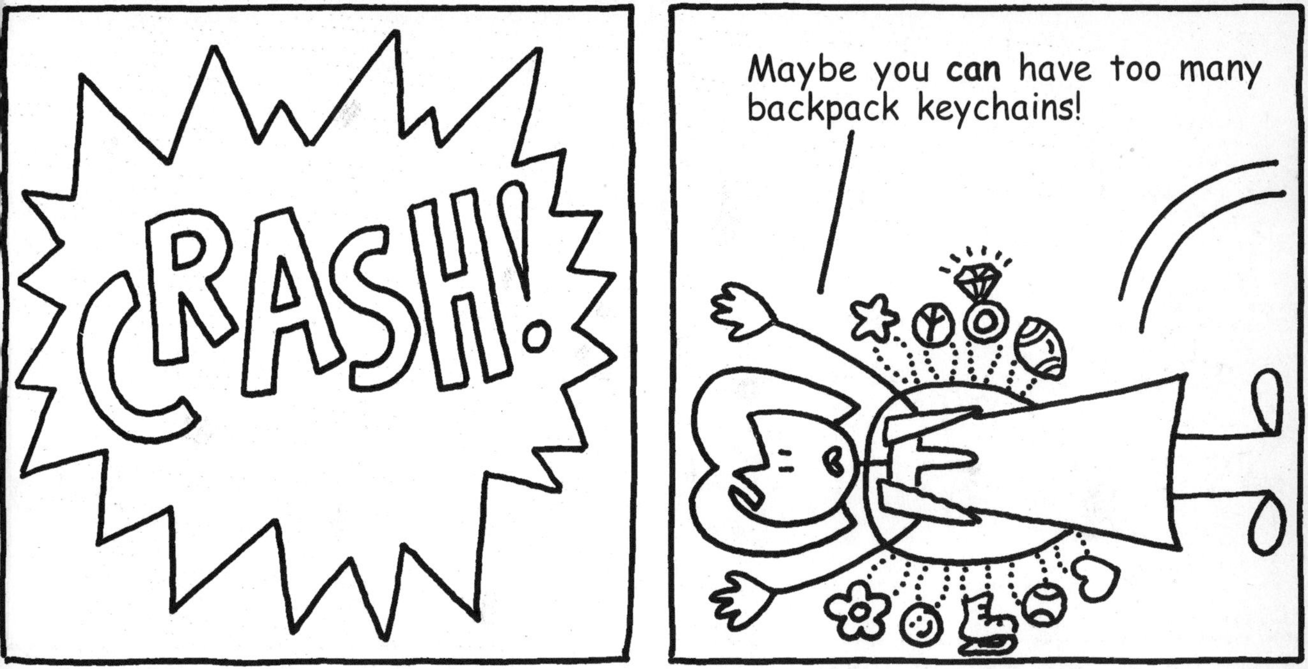
CRASH!
Maybe you **can** have too many backpack keychains!

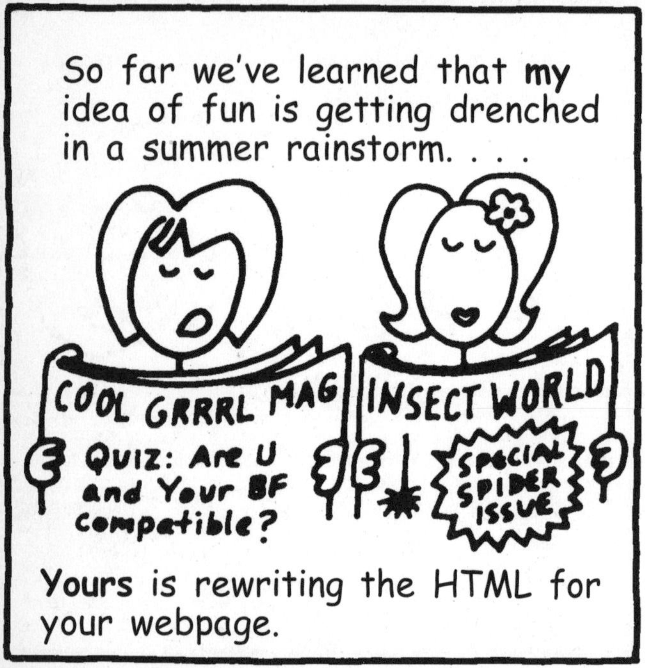
So far we've learned that **my** idea of fun is getting drenched in a summer rainstorm. . . .
COOL GRRRL MAG
QUIZ: Are U and Your BF compatible?
INSECT WORLD
SPECIAL SPIDER ISSUE
Yours is rewriting the HTML for your webpage.

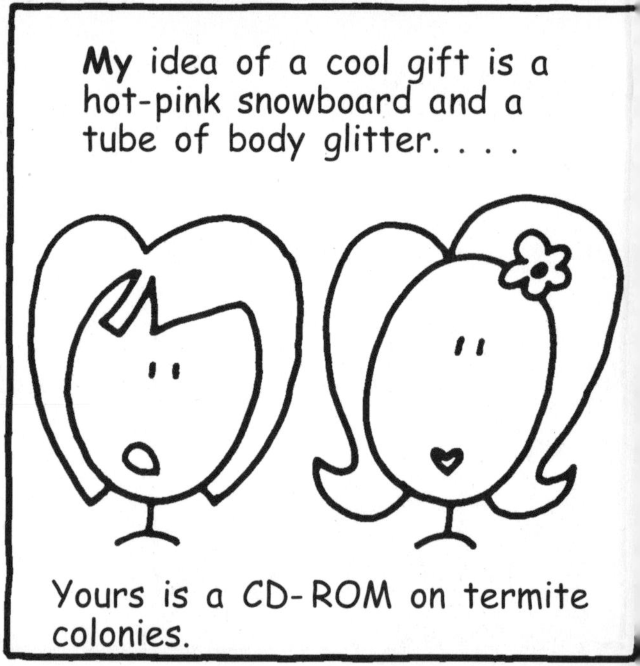
My idea of a cool gift is a hot-pink snowboard and a tube of body glitter. . . .
Yours is a CD-ROM on termite colonies.

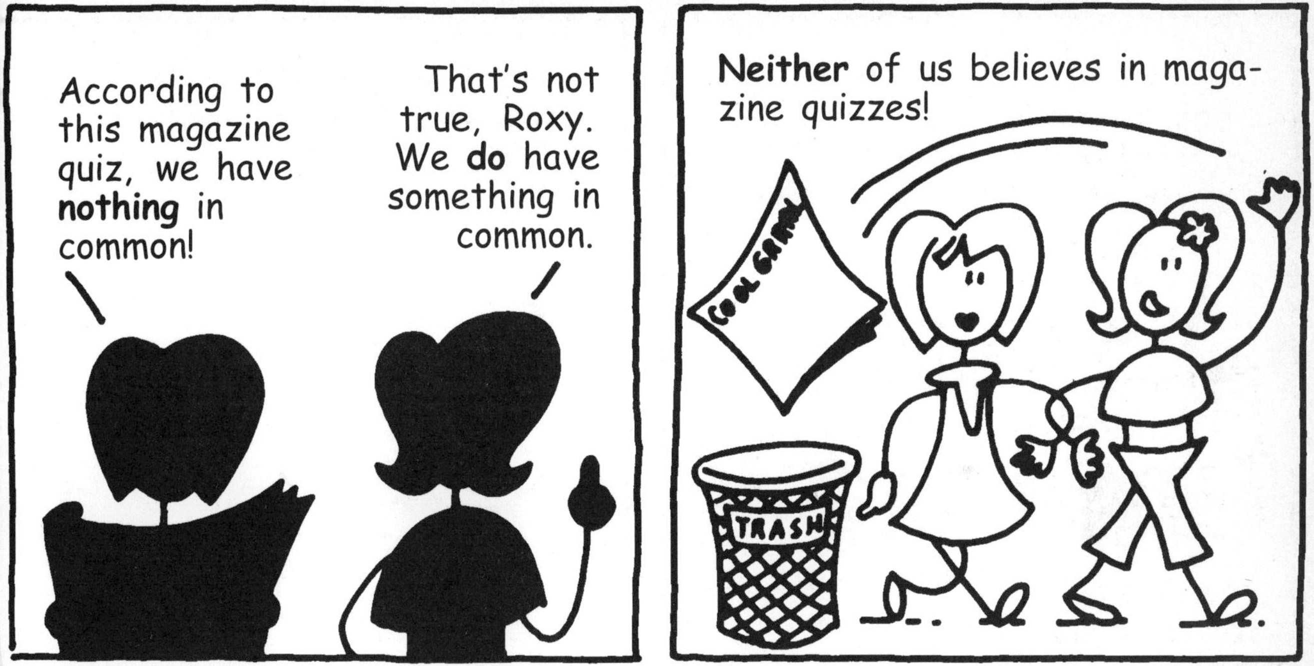
According to this magazine quiz, we have **nothing** in common!
That's not true, Roxy. We **do** have something in common.
Neither of us believes in magazine quizzes!
TRASH

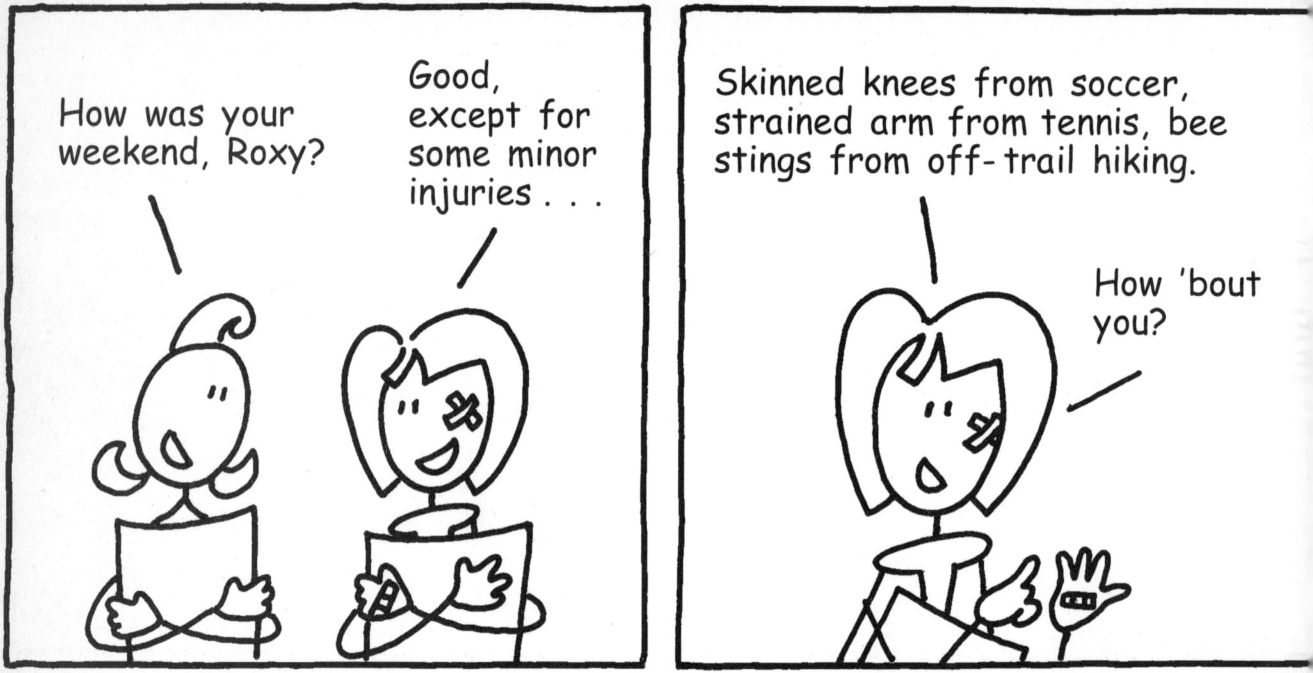
How was your weekend, Roxy?
Good, except for some minor injuries . . .
Skinned knees from soccer, strained arm from tennis, bee stings from off-trail hiking.
How 'bout you?

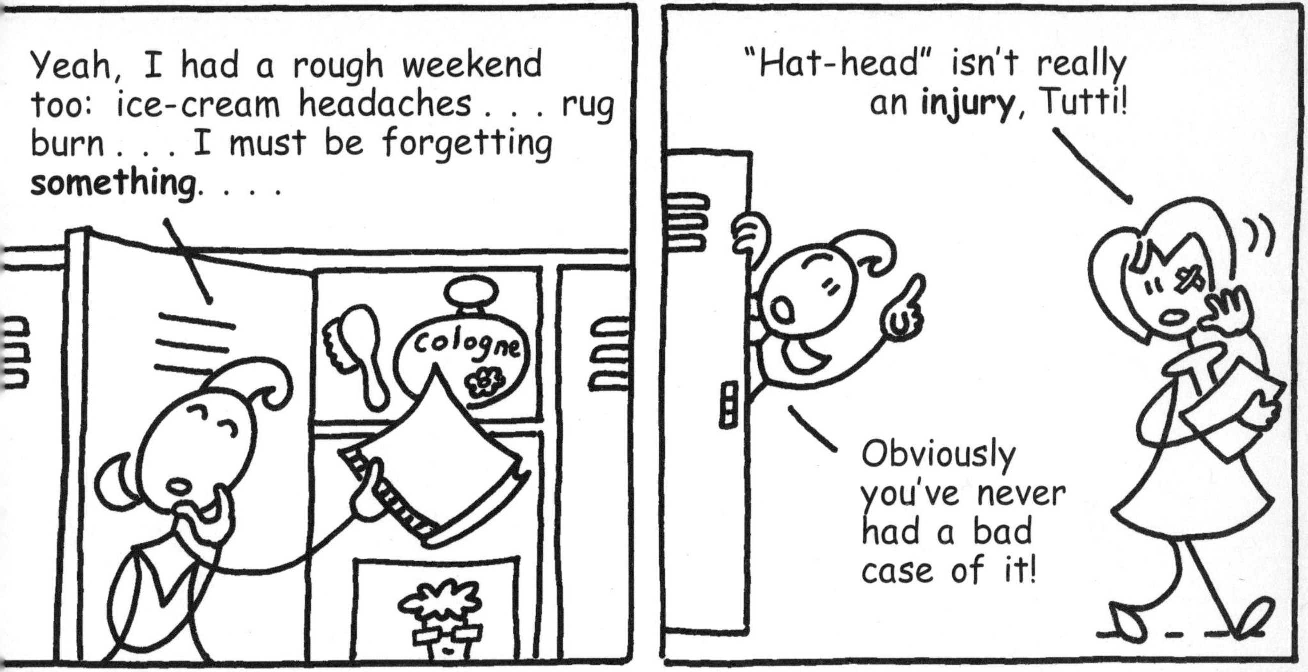
Yeah, I had a rough weekend too: ice-cream headaches . . . rug burn . . . I must be forgetting **something**. . . .
Cologne
"Hat-head" isn't really an **injury**, Tutti!
Obviously you've never had a bad case of it!

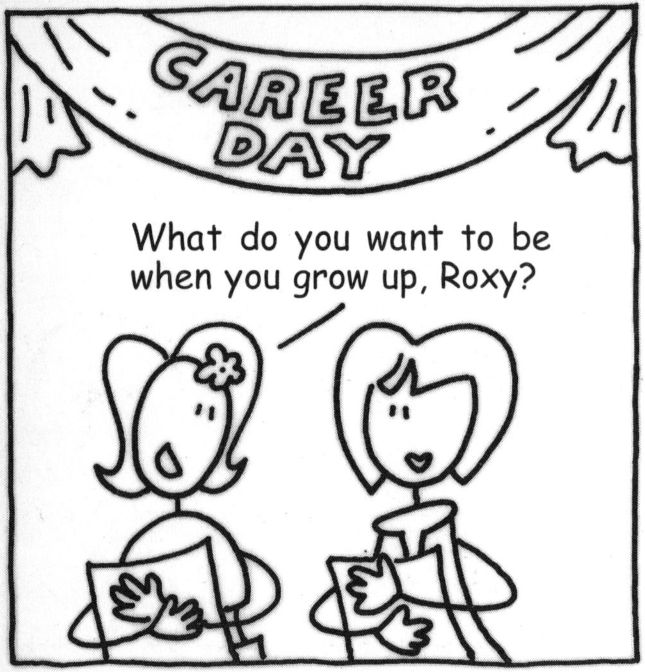
CAREER DAY
What do you want to be when you grow up, Roxy?

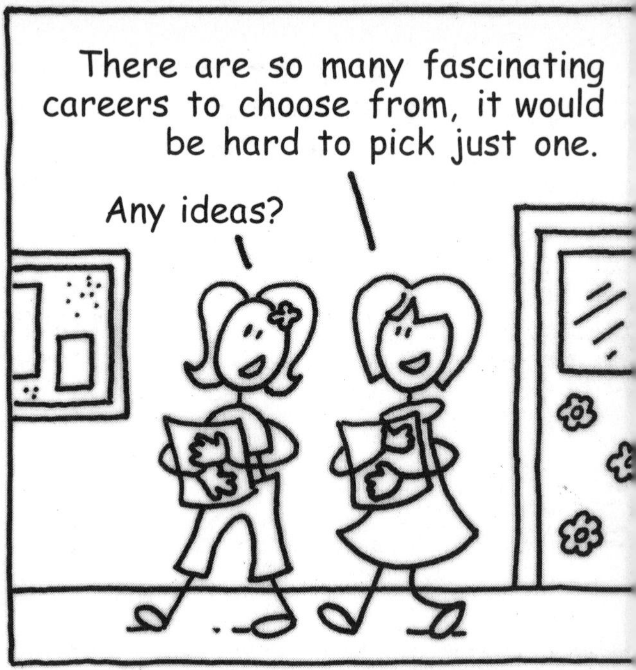
There are so many fascinating careers to choose from, it would be hard to pick just one.
Any ideas?

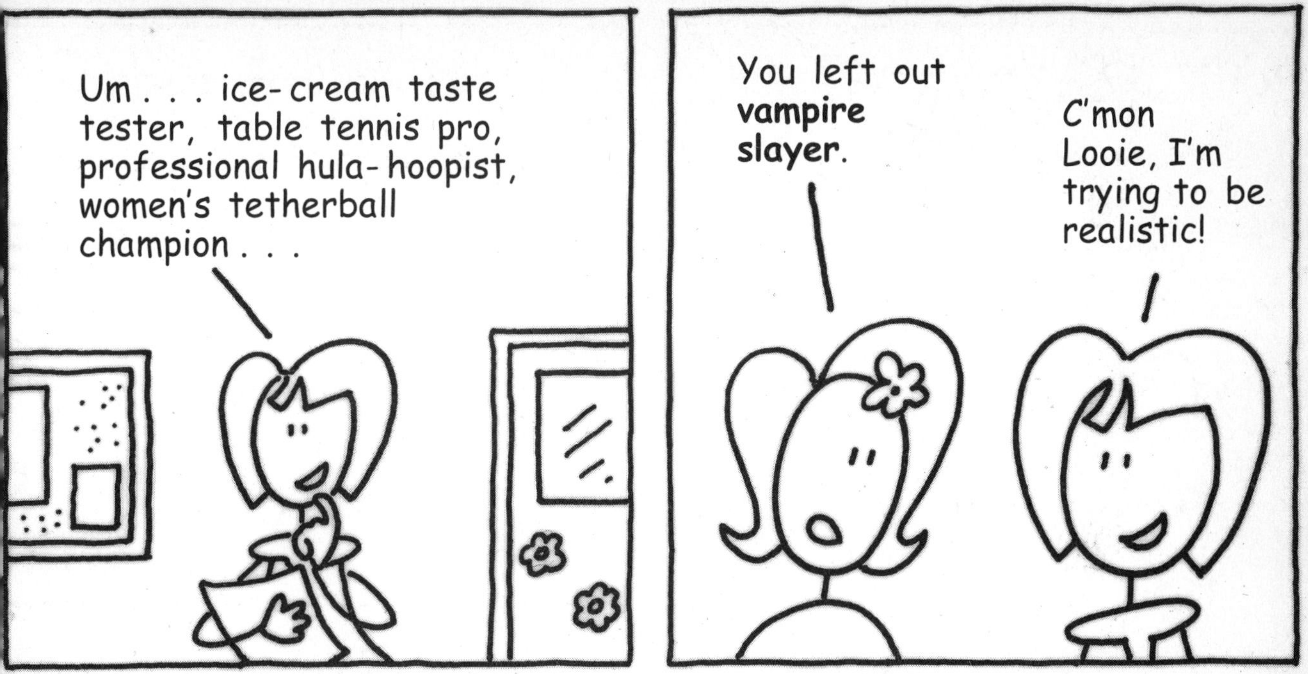
Um . . . ice-cream taste tester, table tennis pro, professional hula-hoopist, women's tetherball champion . . .
You left out **vampire slayer**.
C'mon Looie, I'm trying to be realistic!

ISBN 0-439-34057-8
Copyright © 2002 by 2 GRRRLS, Inc.
Design by Louise Bova

Published by Scholastic Inc. All rights reserved.

12 11 10 9 8 7 6 5 4 3 2 1   2 3 4 5 6/0
Printed in the U.S.A.
First Scholastic printing, October 2002